# The Joy of it All

a novel

# KARA JEFFERIES

Reader Advisory: This work contains themes related to death.

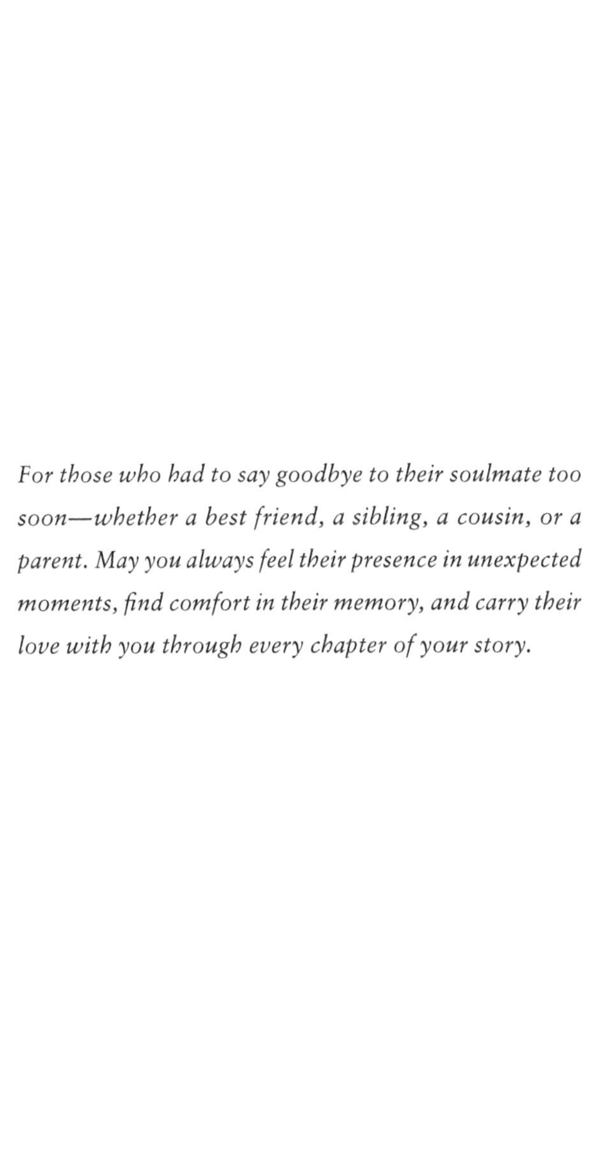

*For those who had to say goodbye to their soulmate too soon—whether a best friend, a sibling, a cousin, or a parent. May you always feel their presence in unexpected moments, find comfort in their memory, and carry their love with you through every chapter of your story.*

# Prologue

## HAZEL

I always assumed that when I had to speak at a funeral, it would be for my Grandma or Grandpa. I never once thought it would be for my cousin. I always tell myself I'm not my mom, but the similarities are frightening. When my mom was only eighteen, she had to stand before family and strangers to speak at her cousin's funeral. He died at only eighteen. I am twenty-three years old, speaking at my cousin's funeral. I have no idea why this happened to Olivia, but I'm afraid if I dwell on it too long, I'll lose myself to grief.

My dad grabs my knee and squeezes it, his way of telling me it's my time to speak about Olivia. Slowly, I stand and shimmy my way past my dad, mom, and Hayes to get to the main aisle. Hayes grabs my hand, prompting me to look down at him. He gives me a reassuring nod, but it does nothing to calm my nerves.

The microphone is attached to a tall walnut-colored podium. As I lower it to accommodate my five-foot-three-inch height, it makes a high-pitched screeching noise. As I prepare to speak, I take a deep breath, but my throat feels as though I'm trying to swallow shards of broken glass.

"Have you been in a rainstorm where the rain falls so slowly from the sky you can see the path it takes from heaven only for the rain to instantly become so fierce that you're forced to take cover or become overtaken by the wrath of the storm? That's what watching your best friend die feels like."

I hear Kadin crying in the row opposite my parents and look over to her only for a second because I can't allow myself to start crying and not finish what I have to say.

"Memories of your childhood play through your head in slow motion. Most of them are fun and force you to smile; they make you feel lighter and make breathing easier, but they're quickly overtaken by ones that break your heart for the memories you'll never make as adults."

My Aunt Joy is sobbing in the front row, and my Uncle Xavier is just staring past me. His usually bright blue eyes, which remind everyone of a summer sky, are now grey like a cold wintery day. He pulls my aunt closer to him, trying to console her, but she's too far gone. Nolen and Jensen, Olivia's twin brothers, sit side by side, their shoulders slumped as if carrying an invisible weight. Despite their usual brotherly banter, today, they're shadows of themselves. Nolen's light-brown hair is tousled from him pushing his hand through it. Jensen's jaw is clenched, his usually bright eyes now dark and downcast. Both of them stare at their feet, faces blank and void of emotion.

I continue, "Saturdays were Olivia's favorite. She'd wake up early and eat some form of protein, so she was ready for a day of softball or a day watching Kadin play soccer. Olivia always took care of herself, and she loved to be around people. She was the baby of the three of us, almost a year younger than Kadin and I, but she did everything she could not to be left behind. She graduated a year early from high school, and she played softball better than all the girls her age.

When Olivia set her mind to something, there was zero chance of changing it. And that didn't change when she found out she was sick. She made a list: move home, get married, have her baby, and then die. She knew this day was coming, and she was going to be in control of it. She refused to let her illness control her or her decisions. Olivia accomplished more in the last two years than most people do in a lifetime. I'm just so fortunate that I was by her side to experience all her successes with her."

Without looking up, I grab my speech, which I never even bothered to glance at, and walk to where Olivia is lying in her coffin. It's closed, and I'm so thankful for that. I grab a pink chrysanthemum and place it on top of it as I slowly run my palm across the lid. It's cold and hard, just like one would imagine, but I guess in that moment of desperation, I was hoping for a sign from God. Maybe a sign that she was okay, that she was happy and out of pain.

Over the past several weeks, I've been pleading with a God that I'm not sure I even believe in. So, for me to stand here today looking for the sign is the definition of insanity.

Losing all sense of time, I stand over her coffin, my hand resting there until my dad gently guides me back to my seat. The rest of the service blurs together in my memory as Kadin's speech seamlessly transitions into Jett's, followed by a few words from our other high-school friends. The twins remain silent, avoiding eye contact with friends and family. My mom thanks everyone at the end on behalf of 'the family' as the ceremony draws to a close.

# Chapter 1

## KADIN

High-School Graduation

For the past four years, I woke up early and stayed up all night studying for finals, all leading to this moment. It felt like today would never happen, but here I am, standing on the precipice of a new chapter. The past seemed like a relentless cycle of early mornings and sleepless nights, each day blending into the next with the singular purpose of reaching this milestone: graduation.

My phone buzzes on my vanity, pulling my attention from my mirror. Without looking down, I slide the notification and open FaceTime.

"Are you riding with us?" Hazel asks as she makes an 'O' with her mouth while putting on mascara in her vanity mirror.

"No, I told you already I'm riding with Jett."

"Kadin, it's our last day of high school; the three of us have to go together."

"Sorry," I say, not waiving from my convictions. Jett and I have walked onto campus together on the first and the last day of school since kindergarten, and today is no different. I'm not going to change my mind. "I'll see you and Olivia at our normal meeting spot."

"Ugh!" she growls into the phone. "You're impossible."

"Why aren't you driving with Hayes?" I can't help but to ask. It's a simple question, but it's loaded for me.

"I am. He's picking Olivia and me up. Why are you asking about Hayes?" Irritation laces her question.

"It just means we're finally (almost) out of high school, and maybe it's time you and Hayes stop playing games."

"I have to go."

That's all I get before she blows me a kiss and hangs up. I stare at the blank screen, a smile tugging at my lips. Classic Hazel, constantly dodging anything that has to do with Hayes Emmerson. I can't help but wonder if she'll admit just how much she's always loved him. They've both been my best friends forever and yet, here we all are, stuck in this weird limbo where they blissfully deny their feelings for each other.

And me? I've always loved Jett – probably more than I should. But I'll never say it. I can't say anything now; after all this time, it would ruin everything. So, I keep it to myself, watching him fall for someone else, knowing I'll never be the one for him. It's easier this way...

There's a honk outside my house, and I run downstairs, jumping to the landing and skipping the last two stairs.

"You're going to break your damn ankle one day doing that, and you won't be able to play soccer." My mom scolds me.

I love soccer, but I wonder if she loves it more than I do.

I kiss her on the cheek. "Last day. I'll see you when I get home."

"Remember, after graduation, we're all going to dinner together." When my mom says *we're all* going to dinner, that means Hazel and her parents, Olivia and her parents along with her twin brothers, my parents and four siblings, Jett and his parents, and Hayes's family. It's excessive with at least twenty people.

"Yeah, I know. The five of us are coming straight from graduation, so we'll meet you there. You're acting like I won't see you after graduation for pictures," I tease, rolling my eyes with a playful grin.

"Oh yeah, I guess I forgot that part," my mom says, a hint of nostalgia in her voice.

I dash down the few steps of our walkway and then look back up at her. She's still stood at the door, leaning against the frame, watching me with a mix of pride and bittersweet emotions flickering across her face.

"Mom, I'll see you later, okay?" I say with a grin before jumping into the passenger seat of Jett's car, feeling the familiar rush of excitement.

While the door is still open, Jett leans across me and shouts, "Good morning, Mrs. Johnston!"

"Call me Roxanne!" she calls back, a smile breaking through her wistfulness.

And with that, Jett and I drive away, the car humming with the same energy that has carried us through the past few years of high school. The sun continues rising, casting a golden glow over the neighborhood as we head toward the final chapter of high school.

"Are you excited?" I ask, turning in my seat to face Jett.

"For graduation? For high school to be done? Or to play football in Texas?" He glances at me with his goofy grin. His words are light, but they always carry an effortless charm that makes him the center of attention. I watch him for a moment, feeling that familiar frustration bubble up. How does he not see it? I've been by his side through everything, his highs, his lows, and every moment in between. Yet, somehow, I'm invisible in the crowd of people who adore him. Maybe that's the problem. I've been too familiar for too long, and he'll never notice what's right in front of him.

"Any, all of the above, I guess?" One of these days, I'll muster the courage to tell him how I feel. But for now, I'll keep playing the part of the supportive best friend, hoping that someday, he'll look past five-year-old Kadin standing at the bus stop with her mom or seven-year-old Kadin with messy hair throwing him the football for hours until the streetlights came on.

"Yes, yes, and yes." He pauses, his eyes lighting up with excitement. "Wait, was that everything? I feel like I'm forgetting something."

I make my best effort to let him off the hook. "Okay, I get it. You're excited."

We stop at a red light, and he faces me, his dimple on full display. "Kadin, college is going to be amazing. I'm going to get drafted; you'll get scouted to play soccer in some European county, and our dreams will finally come true."

I just smile back at him because he's right; that's all we've ever wanted. I play soccer in Europe, and he plays football here in the States, but there's still a part of me that wonders if I would give up soccer to stay here with him if he ever asked me to.

• • •

As I walk across the stage to receive my diploma, a mix of excitement and trepidation bubbles inside me. The end of high school is not just an end but a beginning—a fresh start in the uncharted territory of college life. The future stretches out before me like an open road, filled with endless possibilities and unknown challenges.

I look out into the crowd and spot my parents and their best friends, their faces beaming with pride. My heart swells with a mixture of gratitude and nervous anticipation. This is the beginning of our next chapter, and I can't help but wonder what lies ahead.

The sun shines brightly on this pivotal day, casting its signature golden glow over the ceremony. The air is filled with the hum of excitement, and the scent of freshly cut grass mingles with the perfume of blooming flowers. As my classmates and I toss our caps into the air, a surge of exhilaration sweeps over me. This is it. The moment we've all been waiting for.

But as I step off the stage, diploma in hand, a thought lingers in the back of my mind: What comes next? College looms on the horizon, a daunting and exhilarating prospect. New faces, new challenges, new everything. The familiar routine of high school is behind me, and ahead lies a world of possibilities.

Will our fivesome always be as tight as we are now? Will Hayes and Hazel end up married or hate each other? Who will Jett marry, and will I like her? I've got to like her because I can't imagine a future without Jett being part of it. Will I play professional soccer, and will Jett play professional football? There are so many unknowns as we walk into the next phase of life.

I take a deep breath, savoring the mix of fear and excitement that churns within me. Today marks the end of one chapter and the beginning of another. And I can't wait to see where this new journey will take me.

# Chapter 2

## HAZEL



FRESHMAN YEAR OF COLLEGE

"You'd never know you're not the oldest child by the way you take control and boss everyone around," Kadin says.

Olivia shakes her head in agreement as they both pick up Kadin's boxes and carry them to her new room.

"Ha, ha. I just want all of us unpacked and ready for tonight," I retort.

Kadin and Olivia are both the 'oldest children' in their families, which means nothing to me because I'm the 'only' child. Those two wear their title like a badge of honor as I do mine. They feel partially responsible for being an example for their younger siblings, responsible for picking up the slack around the house. A responsibility I'm so thankful wasn't bestowed upon me.

"What's tonight?" Kadin's mom, Roxanne, asks as her eyebrows lift, a subtle furrow appearing between them as she tilts her head.

"Just a welcome party at the football house Jett is living at. We were all invited," I answer, feeling utterly oblivious to the disappointed expressions spreading across the dads' faces. I catch them glaring at me, but I shrug it off, not quite sure what I did to spark their disapproval.

My Aunt Roxanne puts her hands on her hips. "Hazel, you're aware that Lincoln University is a D1 school known not only for their academics but their sports programs as well, and if Kadin is going to play professional soccer, partying through college will not be an option."

That is all one-hundred percent true. However, she left out that Lincoln University is also the top party school in Texas, so we will have to participate in a few extracurricular activities.

Kadin is carefree and lighthearted off the soccer field, but once she steps onto the pitch, it's all business. Her goal is to play for a women's European football team, and just like Olivia, when she sets her mind to something, she'll make it happen. So, a few parties here and there will not derail her goal of becoming a professional soccer player.

"I know, Aunt Roxy; I promise I'll keep her on a tight leash just after tonight's welcome party. Okay?" I ask in a sheepish tone.

My Aunt Joy takes this opportunity to chime in, "You know none of you are twenty-one, so technically, none of you should be drinking. And Olivia is barely eighteen."

You'd never know Olivia is younger than Kadin and me; she's more intelligent, taller, and just an all-around better person. Everyone who meets her loves her. She is more mature than the two of us combined.

"Who said anything about drinking? All I said is we were meeting Jett at the football house to make new friends." I hold up my hand to my mom for a high-five, and she just shakes her head at me and whispers so only she and I can hear.

"Listen, camp director. I have to deal with your Aunt Joy and Roxy while you're away. Please don't do anything stupid. You always get yourself into trouble, and you're always the ringleader. Can't you just let someone else make their parents look bad for once?"

"Hey, I take offense to that." Placing an exaggerated hand over my heart. "I'm not a troublemaker; I'm a trouble fixer."

My mom tilts her head, almost resting it on her left shoulder as she rolls her eyes at me, obviously not buying my line of bullshit.

I am just like my mom: outspoken, a tiny bit controlling, and a natural-born saleswoman. I want everything to be perfect for everyone around me, so I prefer to handle details myself, even if I have to use my influence skills to make it happen.

Today is drop-off day. Our freshman year at Lincoln University, just outside of Dallas, Texas, is about to begin in a few days, and it's still surreal that all five of us ended up here together. If I'm being honest, the only reason our parents were comfortable with us leaving California for college was that Jett and Hayes were coming with us. Jett, of course, got recruited to play football, so it made sense for the rest of us to follow.

Kadin's dream of playing D1 soccer perfectly aligns with Lincoln, especially since they've won the NCAA Women's College Cup two years in a row. Hayes wants to coach or work in sports, and with Lincoln's strong focus on athletics, it's a perfect school for him, too. He's taking everything from broadcasting to sports marketing—if it's got 'sports' in the title, he's enrolled.

As for Olivia and me—we didn't care as much about the destination or what the school offered; we just knew we wanted to stay together. Honestly, I still don't even know what I want to do after college, but I guess I'll figure that out later.

Our parents got the four of us a small house right off campus, while Jett will be living in the football house. The place isn't huge, but we each have our own bedrooms. Kadin, Olivia, and I will share a bathroom, and Hayes will have his own.

The house itself is older, built in the early eighties, with large windows and a red brick exterior—a far cry from the modern homes we grew up in back in California. Inside, the living room flows seamlessly into the kitchen, creating an open space perfect for hosting friends without feeling cramped or overwhelmed.

Today is our first day, and the heat is dreadful—Texas summers are much different than in California. The sun seems more intense, and the air is thicker, but somehow, I don't mind, and I've already fallen in love with the state – the sprawling skies, the wide streets, and the undeniable Southern charm. It's different, but it's already home.

The idea of me leaving California for college was unthinkable to my mom. For years, it was an adamant 'over my dead body,' but I've always known I needed to get away, if only for a season. In California, I'm one kind of person; I'm Gabe and Harper's only child, and in our tight-knit community, it wasn't always easy. We don't live in a small town, but it often feels like one because everyone knows everyone, primarily through sports and school. People see me as their daughter first, not as my own person. In California, I'm defined by who my parents are. But in Texas, I can be whoever I choose to be. I'm dying to see the world through my own eyes. Not through the rose-colored lenses my parents have always shown me. Don't get me wrong—I've had a picture-perfect childhood with loving parents and close-knit family and friends. But sometimes, I long for the freedom to make my own mistakes and to experience life without my mom's watchful eyes on me. Just once, I'd like to taste a bit of trouble and adventure on my own terms.

A few hours later, everyone's rooms are unpacked, and the boxes have been broken down and set out by the curb for Monday pick-up. The house is now starting to feel like a home. The scent of fresh paint and new furniture lingered in the air as we walked through each room, marveling at how everything had come together.

All our dads stood in the living room, admiring their interior design skills, sharing a moment of quiet satisfaction. The rooms echoed with the sounds of new beginnings, laughter, and the promise of memories yet to be made.

It was time to say goodbye. The dads exchanged proud smiles, each knowing they had contributed to creating the space where their kids would spend the next four years.

"Mom, I'll be fine. You need to go to the airport before you miss your flight."

I speak into my mom's unruly blonde hair as she holds me in such a tight embrace that I'll be plucking her hair from my teeth for weeks. She pulls herself away and sulks as she walks to my dad, only to quickly change her mind and wrap her body around me like a koala around a eucalyptus tree in a storm. I lift my head, angling it to the sky, and call to my dad.

"Dad, some help here, please." I draw out the last part of 'please' for dramatic effect. "Can you get your wife off me? I can't breathe."

My dad gently removes her arms from my neck and whispers in her ear, "Harper, it's time."

Just those three words send a cascade of tears down my mom's face, which in turn triggers Kadin's mom, Roxanne's tears, and in a typical domino effect, Olivia's mom, my Aunt Joy's eyes flood.

"Strength in numbers," my mom whispers in Hayes's ear as she hugs him goodbye. Fighting back tears, she says, "Take care of my baby, Hayes. Keep her safe. Don't let anyone hurt her."

"Mom! Enough!" I shout. I give Haye's mom a hug and then my Aunt Roxy before I work my way down the line of crying mothers and proud dads until I get to my dad.

He pulls me in for a hug, and I whisper, "Take care of Mom. She's going to be an emotional wreck, then she'll be a worried mess, and that's all before you make it home tonight. The seven stages of grief are real, Dad."

"I will," he whispers back, still holding me.

"Are you going to be okay without me?" I ask.

Dad chuckles, and I feel his strong chest rumble against me. My dad is just over six feet tall, and my mom is almost as tall as him. I, on the other hand, stopped growing just over five feet. I literally got the short end of the stick. Everyone says I'm the perfect blend of my parents. My dad's dark features and almost black eyes are a stark contrast to my mom's bright green ones. I landed somewhere in between with hazel eyes – hence the name. His hair is dark brown, hers is blonde (with a bit of help from the salon), and mine is a light brown that balances them out. I'm the goldilocks between their extremes.

"I was born to handle your mom, Hazel," he says, holding back so much emotion that I don't think he realizes the extent of his hold on me.

I take a deep breath, nod in agreement against his chest, and say, "Better you than me, Dad. I love you and hope you're still alive when I come home for the holidays."

A genuine laugh rumbles from him, which draws my mom's attention from Roxanne, and she says, still wiping tears from her eyes, "Are you two making fun of me?"

In unison, we say, "Nope, just saying goodbye."

I push my dad away as I say, "Go, old man. You're going to get us in trouble, and you're the only one going home with her this time."

My mom walks over and nudges her way under my dad's arm; he pulls her in close to his side.

"Harper, she'll be fine. You've given her a good foundation; she knows right from wrong. She's got this."

Tears fill my eyes, and I strain so hard not to let them fall because once one tear falls, the whole fucking dam is going to break, and I can't do that in front of my parents because if I do, they'll put me on the next flight back to California with them.

Hayes walks over to where I'm standing with my parents, rests his arm across my shoulders, and casually extends his hand to my dad.

"Mr. Jones, I promise to take care of Hazel."

My dad shakes his hand as he looks at me, and with a wink, he says, "Good to hear because if you don't, I'm coming after you, Hayes."

I roll my eyes and share an all-knowing look with my dad. I think one of my favorite things about growing up will always be watching how in love my parents are. My dad has unknowingly set my standards for a boyfriend, let alone my husband, higher than I'm afraid any man can reach. My parents are affectionate with each other; they laugh together and poke fun at each other.

Hayes and I have always just been friends, or at least that is what he claims. But there was a time when my thoughts were consumed by him. It was our sophomore year of high school when we attended homecoming together. I was ecstatic, and the night started out perfectly with flowers, pictures, a party bus, and a fight. Yep, Hayes ruined our night when he saw Elliot and me dancing together.

The night spiraled downhill quickly after the fight. Although the school administration never disciplined the guys involved in the altercation, I didn't keep it a secret from my parents. I've always been open with them, so there was no reason to keep this a secret. My dad wasn't pleased because Hayes and I weren't dating at the time, and he didn't appreciate the controlling vibe Hayes displayed toward me. Hayes always told me I was the right girl at the wrong time, but my dad's rebuttal was, "If you're the right girl, the time will never be wrong."

The four of us stand there on our porch as we watch all our parents drive away in their large black rental van. I'm flooded with a million different emotions again, and for the second time today, I fight back tears. I'm struck with an overwhelming sense of excitement to be on my own for the first time. There's a nervousness about school, uneasiness about living with Hayes, and worry that I may die of starvation without my mom cooking breakfast and dinner for me.

Kadin's loud "woo-hoo" snaps me out of my thoughts. I glance over to see her doing a quirky, happy dance, waving a flyer in the air while chanting, "Party, Party, Party."

# Chapter 3

## HAZEL

Sophomore Year of College

The Texas sun assaults my senses when I roll over toward my window; its intensity is so much sharper and unforgiving compared to the soft, golden light I grew up with in California. The sunlight in Texas is different – harsher, almost blinding, and today, I am definitely not a fan of it.

"Ugh, no," I whine at my open blinds as I roll my body away from the window and the relentless light. "Welcome to your sophomore year." I'm careful in my movements, trying not to slosh the excessive amount of alcohol we drank last night when we baptized our sophomore year.

Once I'm comfortable and confident I won't throw up, I reach out to grab one of my extra pillows and notice I'm not alone.

"Kadin, is that you? Why did you sleep in here and not in your room?"

A hand touches my face, and I quickly realize it's not Kadin's. It's a guy's hand, and I know my boyfriend, Benson, doesn't get back from football camp until tomorrow—and he and

I have never slept together, so naturally, panic erupts in my stomach, and I open one eye slowly as if I'm watching a horror film unfold in my bedroom.

"Hayes!" I shout, my voice a mix of shock and frustration. "What the hell? What are you in doing here?"

He grins sheepishly, rubbing the back of his neck, and my mind races, trying to piece together the hazy memories of last night's party. The relief I should feel that it's Hayes and not some random guy is overshadowed by a growing sense of unease. I can't ignore the tension simmering beneath the surface, the way his presence always feels like a spark ready to ignite when we're alone.

"Seriously, Hayes?" I say, my voice trembling with a mix of anger and something else I can't quite name. "You scared the hell out of me."

His shoulders slump slightly, and his gaze softens as he meets my eyes. "I'm sorry," he says, his voice low. "I didn't mean to freak you out." He pauses and scrubs his hand over his face." I'll go if you want."

For a moment, I'm torn between telling him to leave and asking him to stay, the unexpected intimacy of the situation making my pulse quicken. The needling thought of *'is it for real this time'* toys with me.

Hayes rolls to his back, putting one arm over his head, and says, "Damn, I missed this, Hazel, you were so good last night."

He makes this weird humming sound, and that's all it takes for the gallon of alcohol I consumed last night to shoot straight up from my stomach. I launch myself out of bed and grab my trash can just in the nick of time. And, yep, there it is. Not only did I have sex with Hayes last night, but I just vomited in front of him.

He grins, his eyebrows lifting with a mock offense as he

props himself up on one elbow, a hand resting over his chest in dramatic fashion. "Well, that's a first," he says, his voice light with amusement. "I've never had a girl physically ill at the sight of me in bed with them in the morning." His grin widens, and with a playful glint in his eye, he adds, "You've always had a special talent for bruising my ego, Hazel."

"Go away, Hayes," I say between dry heaves and coughing fits.

Hayes jumps from the bed, comes over to me, and wraps my long, light brown hair into a black scrunchie he grabbed from my desk.

"Ugh fuck," I groan. "I think I'm dying this time."

His laugh rains down on me like a summer storm as he stands over me, rubbing my back. "You're not dying," he assures me.

I lower myself to my knees, pushing the vomit-filled trashcan away from me and burying my head in my hands.

"Hazel, it's no big deal; why are you so embarrassed? We've all been here. We partied too much last night. We welcomed in our sophomore year in style. A hangover well deserved if you ask me," he says, trying to convince me not to crawl into a hole and die.

"Hayes, I cheated on my boyfriend last night. I can't do this with you right now. Can you give me space?" I ask through my hands.

"Hazel, it's just Ben; you guys weren't serious anyway."

"Yeah, because you always do everything in your power to make sure I never get serious about another guy. Just go!" I shout.

Hayes's expression shifts instantly, his brow furrowing and his lips pressing into a tight line. His eyes soften as they look into mine, scanning my face as though he's trying to read what's really going on beneath the surface. "Are you sure you're okay?" he asks, his voice low, filled with worry.

I take a deep breath, trying to steady my racing heart and queasy stomach. "Yeah, I'm fine," I reply, though my voice betrays the lingering shock and confusion. I glance towards the door, my mind a whirlwind of emotions.

Hayes hesitates for a moment. His hand lingers in the air as if he wants to reach out and comfort me, but he holds back, respecting my space for once.

"I'm really sorry," he says again, his voice filled with remorse. "If you need anything, just let me know. I'll be in my room."

I point to the door. He nods, understanding, and quietly leaves the room, the door closing behind him.

As the silence envelops me, I sink back into my pillow, my mind replaying the events of the morning. The room feels strangely empty now, but the tension slowly begins to dissipate. I take a few deep breaths, trying to collect my thoughts and calm my nerves.

Hayes and I have never been on the same page. He's only concerned about me when someone else shows interest in me. Hayes is the literal definition of a cock blocker.

If a guy shows interest in me, Hayes scares him off. And when I say he scares him off, I'm not exaggerating. Hayes is six-foot-four inches tall, with a full head of unruly blond hair and green eyes that change color as quickly as leaves turn in the fall. His eyes shift from bright green to deep emerald, depending on what he wears, and he is built like a Roman god. But it's not just his appearance that intimidates them. He'll casually slip into conversation that we've been best friends since childhood, drop hints about our shared history, and subtly plant seeds of doubt. He'll ask pointed questions about the guy's future plans or make sarcastic comments that are just sharp enough to make them feel uneasy. Oh, and let's not forget his favorite one about how my dad personally asked him to 'keep an eye on me.' It's like a game to him – he doesn't even have to be physical; he's already won by the time the guy realizes they don't stand a chance or he's too much of an obstacle.

Hayes is an athlete who always performs at the highest level, training every day. The only time I see him cheat on his diet is with alcohol. No sweets, no coffee…no fun! When I get clinging or sentimental, I remind myself Hayes Emmerson and I would never work for just those key reasons alone.

My mom swears we'll end up together, but after fifteen years of chasing after him and waiting on him, I know now that I'm a thing of convenience for him; I'm a possession. I'm what he wants when there's no one else around or, again, when someone else wants me.

Later that day, I decide it's time to break things off with Benson. The weight of guilt is too much to bear, and I know dragging this out will only make things worse. I invite him over to my place, hoping to end things with as little pain as possible.

When he arrives, there's a smile on his face, eyes lighting up, unaware of the stress eating at me. He steps into the living room, his usual warmth filling the space, but it's short-lived. As soon as I sit down, his smile falters, confusion replacing it as he senses the shift in my demeanor.

"Benson, we need to talk," I begin, my voice wavering despite my best efforts to keep it steady.

His eyes flicker, his expression tightening as concern transforms into something more guarded. He shifts his weight slightly, his jaw tightening. "Is everything okay?" he asks.

I take a deep breath, trying to steady myself. "No, it's not. I've been thinking a lot, and I realize I can't keep doing this."

He frowns, confusion clouding his eyes. "Doing what? What are you talking about?"

I look down at my hands, unable to meet his gaze. "Us. I can't keep pretending that everything is fine when it's not. I've been lying to myself and to you."

His face falls, and he reaches out to touch my hand, but I pull away. "What do you mean? Did something happen?"

Tears well up in my eyes as I shake my head. "I don't want to go into the details. It's just… I'm not the person you think I am. I made a mistake and don't want to hurt you any more than I already have."

Benson's jaw tightens, and he leans back, crossing his arms over his chest. "Is this about Hayes?"

The mention of Hayes's name hits me like a punch to the gut. I nod slowly, feeling the tears spill over. "Yes, it's always been about Hayes, hasn't it? Deep down, I think we both knew this wasn't going to work because of him."

He lets out a bitter laugh, shaking his head. "I always suspected it, but I hoped I was wrong. I hoped you'd see that *we* could be happy together."

"I'm sorry," I whisper, my voice breaking. "You deserve someone who can give you their whole heart, and that's not me. I thought I could, but I can't." A crushing weight settles in my chest as the words leave my mouth. I wanted this to work between us so badly, for Benson to be the person I ran to with my good news and for me to be the person he needed. But deep down, I knew I would never be that person for him because as long as Hayes is in my life, it'll always be him.

Benson stands up, running a hand through his hair. "I guess that's it then. I wish you'd been honest with me sooner."

"I know, and I'm sorry for that too," I say, standing up to face him. "I never wanted to hurt you. You've been nothing but kind and loving, and you deserve better."

He nods, his eyes filled with a mix of hurt and resignation. "I hope you figure things out, and I hope Hayes is worth it."

With that, he turns and walks out of the door, leaving me standing there with a heart heavier than ever. The silence that follows is deafening, a stark reminder of the mess I've created. Hayes isn't worth it, last night wasn't worth it, everything Benson said is spot-on. There will never be more than games between Hayes and me, and it's time I accept it.

# Chapter 4

## OLIVIA



It's an early Sunday morning. The sun has just begun peering over the horizon, casting a soft golden light through the windows. The house is eerily quiet except for the occasional creak of the floorboards and the distant hum of traffic. Kadin, Hazel, and Hayes left hours ago for Kadin's game, their hurried footsteps and animated chatter as they headed out the door, a tale-tale sign that Kadin hadn't wanted to get out of bed and was running late.

Hazel never misses Kadin's games; her loyalty and enthusiasm for our best friend's success are evident in the way she cheers (rather screams) from the sidelines, at Kadin, at opposing players, at referees, and at other students. Her energy is infectious, and lately, it's clear that Hayes has caught the bug, too. He never misses an opportunity to spend time with Hazel, a stark contrast to his previous aloofness.

I feel guilty about not being there with them. I've used the same excuses over and over—tired, not feeling great—but the truth is, I just don't have the energy. It's like my body is betraying me, and I can't figure out why. I keep telling myself it's nothing, just school stress, but deep down, I can't shake the feeling that something's wrong. But maybe it's no big deal; who knows?

Something shifted between Hazel and Hayes recently. The change is subtle but undeniable. Maybe it's because Hazel has finally stopped chasing him and started dating, her focus shifting from him to other guys. Or maybe Hayes has finally realized what's been right in front of him all along—that he'll never find anyone quite like her. Hazel's laugh, the way her green eyes light up when she talks about something she loves (which, let's be honest, is mostly parties), and the way she fiercely supports her friends and family—that's not something any of us take for granted.

As I sit in the house's stillness, I can't help but reflect on the dynamic between them. Hazel, with her boundless spirit and unyielding determination, has always been a force to be reckoned with. Hayes, on the other hand, has always been the laid-back one, content to go with the flow. But now, there's a new tension that wasn't there before. It's as if they're both teetering on the edge of something new, and only time will tell which way they'll fall.

The simple greeting of "Good Morning" makes me jump five feet in the air.

Clutching my chest to ensure I'm not dying, I look behind me to see Jett standing there with his medium brown hair tousled from sleep. His blue eyes are still a bit hazy but slowly coming to life, and that dimple on his cheek shows as he grins. Even half-awake, his presence lights up the room.

"What are you doing here?" I'm even more panicky now than I was when I thought there was an intruder. At least I could run from an intruder.

"I didn't want to drive back to the football house last night, so I stayed here with Hayes," he says, wearing nothing but grey sweatpants and muscles. He looks sexily mussed, and I'm here for it.

"Don't you think you should share those things with me? Do you know how hard it is for me to sneak around with you, let alone not tell Hazel and Kadin? Oh my God, does Hayes know? Because if Hayes knows, he'll tell Hazel, and then she'll be pissed that she…"

"Calm down, O. You're going to give yourself a heart attack. Seriously, what's the big deal? We're hanging out." He winks at me.

"Did you just wink at me?" I ask, twisting my face in disapproval.

"Not working for you?"

"No. It's not working for me! Jett, we are not hanging out. You and Hayes hang out, you and Hazel hang out. You and I are having sex," I say in a whisper, just in case someone else is hiding in this house.

He walks closer to me and pulls me into him, resting his arms where my ass and back meet. "We are having some really good sex, aren't we?"

"Did you tell Kadin?" I ask, trying to put just a little bit of distance between us.

"No, I told you she won't care. What is the big deal about telling Kadin?"

"Because she likes you, Jett!" I insist.

"She does not like me," he argues, his eyes wide with surprise as if he doesn't believe me.

"You're an idiot, you know that, right? You are oblivious about how Kadin feels for you, and Hayes is oblivious about how Hazel feels about him. At twenty-two years old, you should have good enough instincts to know when someone has been in love with you since elementary school."

"We're best friends."

"And, your best friend has loved you for years, and now we're fucking, and she's my best friend, and this is going to ruin the whole dynamic of our friendship group. I think we should stop this."

His expression falters, eyes narrowing slightly as he stares at me. "Are you serious?" he asks, his voice low and strained, the hurt evident in every word.

"No, I'm not serious." I sigh, defeated because I don't want to stop. I like sneaking around with Jett; it's exciting. I've never done anything remotely close to this, and it's fun and thrilling. I want to see where this goes between us without all our friends interfering, but I also know I owe it to Kadin to be truthful.

I walk to our couch and motion for Jett to sit with me. "I need you to tell Kadin today," I say softly.

Before I can settle into a seat, he gently grabs my hand and pulls me onto his lap, forcing me to straddle him, and it does all sorts of weird things to my body.

"Okay, I'll meet her for lunch after her game today."

# Chapter 5

## KADIN

I throw myself down on the grass and unlace my cleats, pull my socks down, and peel my sweaty shin guards from my shins. I think this is the most disgusting part of playing soccer: sweaty, smelly shin guards. When I was a kid, I would chase the girls around with them, thinking it was funny. A few years older and more mature, I'm aware it's probably the most disgusting thing I've ever done.

I reach in my bag to grab my slides and my phone. There's a text from Jett.

*Jett* – Can you meet for lunch?

There are two things to know about Jett. First, he always texts in complete sentences using proper punctuation, and second, it drives him crazy when I don't. He sent this message an hour ago, but I still text him back, even though he's probably already made other plans.

*Me* – You still hungry

Immediately, he replies.

*Jett* – Is that a question or a statement?

*Me* – either

*Jett* – I'm hungry; I've been waiting for you to eat. Let's meet at Joe's in forty-five minutes, does that work?

*Me* – I'm with Hazel and Hayes

*Jett* – Ditch them.

*Me* – Rude!

*Jett* – See you soon!

I walk over to where Hazel and Hayes are sitting. Hazel immediately jumps from her chair and holds her hand up for a high five. Jett is the only person who has ever hugged me after a game. I secretly hope it's because it's me, but my gut tries to tell me it's because, as bad as I stink, he's used to worse from guys on his team. Maybe his sense of smell is dead after years of football locker rooms. But secretly, it gives me butterflies every time he does it. I missed him today.

"Great game," Hayes says, giving me a fist bump.

"Thanks," I reply.

"Hungry?" Hazel asks, and there's a nervousness that comes over me.

Do I make an excuse to have them take me to the house so I can grab my car, or do I have them drop me off with Jett and tell them he wants to meet with me alone?

Why does he want to meet with me alone? It's been a minute since we've spent any quality time together, and I can't help but wonder if he misses me. My heart races just thinking about it. I've always loved him—ever since we were kids, before I even understood what love really was. He's always been there, a constant in my life, and I've spent years hoping, wishing, that one day he'd see me the way I see him.

I try not to read too much into this, to take it at face value, but I can't help the hope that bubbles up inside me. What if this is my chance? What if he finally sees me? The thought of being alone with him makes my pulse quicken. I've been waiting for a moment like this, and maybe…maybe it's time I finally tell him how much I've always liked him. It's terrifying, but I can't keep this bottled up forever.

I just want him to know. Maybe he feels the same. Maybe he's just waiting for me to say it. I turn my attention back to Hazel and Hayes, who are just staring at me now.

"I'm actually supposed to meet Jett at Joe's," I say, playing with the hem of my shirt. "I was hoping you could drop me off, and I'd just have him give me a ride back to the house when we're done."

Hazel raises an eyebrow, her arms crossing. "So…we're not invited?"

I wince, playing with a rogue strand of hair. "He said just me. I don't know…this was all just over text?" I add with a shrug, not quite meeting their eyes.

"Yeah, we'll drop you off. I'll take Hazel to lunch alone," Hayes says with a slight smirk on his face, his eyes glinting mischievously.

She looks at him side-eye and asks, "Who are you?"

"Let's just go," Hayes says.

In the car on the way over, I try to spray perfume and brush my wet hair. My hair is literally wet from sweat, and I'm doubting every decision leading up to this moment.

"Do I smell?" I ask anyone who's listening.

"Like a toddler who just found her mom's favorite perfume," Hayes deadpans.

I immediately roll down my window and hang my head out, trying to look more windblown than the washing machine.

"Can I ask what's going on?" Hazel says.

"What?"

"Why are you bathing yourself in perfume and hanging your head out the window like one of my mom's dogs? What am I missing?"

"I'm trying not to smell like I just played soccer for three hours. That's it."

"Why don't I believe you?" she says just as Hayes approaches the restaurant.

"Why do I not care," I say before jumping out of the car and slamming the door behind me.

"Hey, don't slam my door," Hayes shouts at me, and I wave at him an apology.

Walking into Joe's never gets old. The smell of fresh bread assaults my senses, and I inhale deeply, savoring it. The warm, yeasty aroma mixed with the sweetness of freshly baked cookies is intoxicating. I'm not sure anything compares to this comforting scent. Joe's setup is similar to an amusement park line. You weave through a maze of pillars to get to the register, where you order and pay. They give you a number, and then a server brings your sandwich to your table.

The interior of Joe's is cozy and inviting, with rustic wooden tables and chairs that have seen their fair share of conversations and laughter. The walls display vintage posters and black-and-white photos of the city from decades past.

I scan the room to see if Jett is here, and sure enough, he is—sitting at our usual table by the window. He's always early, always dependable. He catches my eye and waves me overenthusiastically. I point to the line, letting him know I still need to order, but he mouths, "I ordered for us already."

As I approach the table, he stands up, his tall frame unfolding with ease. He reaches out to hug me, but I hold up my hands to stop him. He looks at me, his face tightened in confusion.

"You may not be able to smell that I just got done playing, but trust me when I say you do not want to hug me."

"Seriously, I play football." He grins and pulls me into a hug, ignoring my protests. His arms wrap around me, and I just melt into him for a second too long. He smells so good, a mix of cedarwood and something distinctly Jett.

"Your hair stinks," he teases, his voice a playful whisper in my ear.

"I tried to warn you," I say, pushing away from him, only for him to pull me back in.

"I'm just kidding. I mean, you do smell, but not bad," he says, laughing.

I shove him away, my cheeks flushing with a mix of embarrassment and amusement, then sit down. The table is already set with napkins, silverware, and our drinks—my favorite iced tea and his usual black coffee.

"So, what did you order?" I ask, trying to shift the focus away from my post-workout state.

"Your favorite: turkey club with extra avocado," he replies, his eyes sparkling with mischief. "And a side of sweet potato fries."

I can't help but smile. Jett always knows just what I need. As we wait for our food, the conversation flows easily, filled with laughter and the kind of banter that only comes from years of friendship.

"So, what do I owe this lunch privilege, just the two of us?" I finally ask, needing to know why he's asked me here.

"Can't a guy take his best friend to lunch and catch up?"

And there it is, *'best friend'*. The truth of those two words hits me like a punch to the gut. That's all I will ever be to Jett—his best friend. I'm the girl who stood at the bus stop, clinging to her mom's leg, terrified to start school, until he took my hand and dragged me behind him up the four steps onto the yellow school bus. The girl who sat next to him daily, sharing secrets and dreams of playing professional sports, never daring to hope for his heart.

"Of course we can; we used to hang out all the time. But lately, with how busy we've all been, we've hardly seen you. So, I just assumed if we were going to hang out, you'd want the whole group here."

"Well, there is one thing I need to talk to you about."

My heart stutters. This will either be the best day of my life or the absolute worst. I lean forward, gripping the edge of the table as I ask, "What?"

He tilts his head slightly, eyes narrowing as if he's trying to decipher something puzzling. "What, what?" he asks.

"What do you need to talk to me about," I repeat, my foot tapping nervously against the floor.

He swallows, and my eyes follow the movement of his Adam's apple as it bobs up and down. I force myself to look away, but my stomach is doing somersaults.

"I'm dating Olivia," he says finally, his voice quieter than before. "She said I had to tell you."

I choke—on nothing. Not water, not my tea, not even my spit. Nope, I choke on his words. I slap my hand to my chest, trying to force the air back into my lungs. "I'm sorry; what did you say?"

"Olivia and I are together. Like together, together."

"Oh my God." That's all I can manage to say. My heart is pounding in my ears, drowning out the conversations from other tables and the clanging of silverware against plates. The world around me fades, enveloping me in a haze of red-hot embarrassment. Or is this rage? Oh, shit, is this what jealousy feels like? I have to get out of here.

The need to escape consumes me, and my mind races with thoughts of an exit plan. How the hell do I leave this restaurant without being too obvious? My palms are sweaty, and heat rises to my cheeks. Every second I stay feels like an eternity, my discomfort intensifying with each passing moment. I glance around, trying to find the least conspicuous route to the door.

I take a deep breath, attempting to steady myself, but my body feels like it's on the verge of betraying me.

"Hey, are you okay? Say something," Jett says as he reaches across the table and grabs my hand.

His touch pulls me from my panic, only to solidify my new reality. Jett and Olivia are together. Today is definitely the worst day of my life.

# Chapter 6

## HAZEL



Senior Year

Tate weaves us through the crowd of people packed into the living room of his house, which he shares with about six other football players. He hardly pauses to give a few teammates fist bumps as he leads us toward the back of the house, heading for his bedroom that he shares with Jett. A line of girls waits by the restroom, their eyes following him shamelessly as he pulls me by the hand.

Tate leads me into his bedroom, shutting the door behind us with a soft click. The room is dimly lit, a quiet contrast to the noise of the house. He smiles as he turns toward me, his eyes soft as he steps closer, brushing a stray piece of hair behind my ear. There's an easiness in the way he moves, like he's always calm, always in control. His hand finds mine, his touch grounding, warm.

I glance around the room—simple, clean, just like Tate. He doesn't have the same chaos swirling around him that I've felt with Hayes. Here, with Tate, things are clear. No guessing, no wondering. Just steady, uncomplicated attention. He makes me feel like I'm the only person in his world, like right now, nothing else matters but us.

Tate's fingers trail down my arm, sending a soft shiver through me. He leans in, lips brushing the side of my neck, and for a moment, I let myself sink into the simplicity of it all. But just as I start to relax, my phone buzzes in my pocket.

I freeze, pulling away slightly to check the screen.

*Of course. Hayes.*

I roll my eyes and mutter under my breath as I swipe at the phone. The guy has impeccable timing – always showing up at the worst possible moment. Times like this just prove to me that Hayes Emmerson has made it his mission to cock black me every chance he gets, and I swear he's somehow perfected the art of it.

Tate steps back, watching me carefully. "Everything okay?"

I nod, shoving the phone back into my pocket, forcing a smile. "Yeah. It's fine."

But it's not. It's never fine when Hayes is involved. No matter how hard I try to move on, he's always there, tugging at the edges of my thoughts, pulling me back into that unspoken magnetic, electric connection we've always had. With Tate, everything is easy and predictable. With Hayes, it's like stepping into a storm. And yet, I can't help but be drawn to him, over and over again.

Tate throws me playfully onto his bed, and I screech, forgetting that half our school is right outside the door. It's already my junior year, and tonight, we won at home, clinching us a spot in the playoffs. Which I've learned for Texas is a *huge* deal. These boys worked for this opportunity their entire lives, different than anything I've ever experienced in California. The amount of commitment it takes to play at this level is impressive.

I lift my own shirt over my head, revealing my matching lace bra that leaves nothing to the imagination. I knew going into tonight that Tate and I were going to celebrate, and I was not going to disappoint him. Tate's eyes scan over my body, and a slight smirk of approval crosses his lips. Before I can say anything else, he's on top of me. His erection digs into my stomach, and my nerves ratchet up several notches. I'm not sure how much longer I can wait for him to make a move before I explode with anticipation or chicken out and run. I've only ever had sex with Hayes, and the few times we did, we were drunk. I know it's not exactly romantic, but that's how it's been between us – intense, fleeting moments fueled by alcohol or jealousy always leaving me confused. It's not what I imagined for my first time (or second, or third) having sex, but somehow, with him, it's always felt like more. Like maybe there is something real buried beneath the chaos, even if he's not willing to admit it. But I'm here with Tate, not Hayes, because he'll never pick me. It's always been that way. So, I settle into the moment with Tate, trying to convince myself that being with someone who wants me and chooses me should be enough.

Tate lowers himself down my stomach, leaving a trail of wetness with his tongue.

"Oh, Tate," I whisper just as his door flies open and bounces back off the wall.

"What the fuck!" he shouts as the lights from the party invade our privacy.

"Oh shit, I'm sorry, Tate. I didn't know you were here." I hear Jett's voice say, and embarrassment fills my body.

"Hazel…is that you?" Jett asks as if I'm not lying here almost naked, with his roommate hovering over me.

"Go away," I demand, trying to position Jett so that some of my currently displayed body will be hidden.

"Hey, Jett." I hear another voice approaching the now-open door, bumping him further into the room.

"Oh hey, Hayes," Jett says, adding as if it's an everyday occurrence, and I'm not half naked.

"We better go; Hazel and Tate are about to, you know what."

I shake my head under Tate and mutter to myself, *'About to do you know what? How old is he?'*

"Hazel?" Hayes questions. "Like my Hazel?"

Tate freezes, his eyes darting between me and Hayes. The lust that was in his eyes just minutes ago is gone, replaced by pure confusion. His mouth opens, then closes, then opens again like he's trying to say something, but the words don't come. He stares at me, blinking, trying to make sense of what just happened.

I push Tate off me, my heart racing as I scramble from the bed. "Get the fuck out, you two!" I shout, shoving both guys out of Tate's bedroom and slamming the door behind them.

But, when I return to Tate, his pants are buttoned, and he's sitting on his bed. And, just like that, Hayes has managed to be a cock blocker yet again.

"I'm not *his* Hazel," I say.

"Then who's Hazel, are you?" he asks me with sarcasm in his voice that doesn't sit well with me.

"I'm no one's, but I was going to allow you to have a piece of me tonight, so I'm a little taken aback by why you're dressed." I sit down next to him and put my hand on his leg.

"Listen, Tate, there's nothing between Hayes and me. He has zero interest in me romantically; he just doesn't like me talking to other guys. It's more of an older brother protector vibe than I'm actually *his* vibe."

Tate narrows his eyes slightly, tilting his head as he studies my face. His jaw tightens, doubt flickering across his expression. His eyes search mine for answers he's not sure he'll get. "You sure?" he asks, his voice low, uncertainty laced in every word.

I turn to him, folding one leg on the bed so I can face him, and nod.

"Hazel." He takes my face in his very large hands that he just used to secure us a spot in the playoffs. "I really like you."

I take a second to digest that. I'm not going to sit here and say I'm unattractive. I'm five foot seven inches, have long, light-brown hair and green eyes, and I'm slender with the perfect botty from years of dance, but Tate Baker is way out of my league, so hearing this is blowing my mind.

"Tate." I kiss his lips. "Hayes." I kiss him again. "Is." Another kiss. "Just a part of my past."

He pulls me to him, and our tongues dance together perfectly. He's perfection. He sucks my lip into his mouth, and I melt into him.

• • •

I wake up to Tate peppering my bare shoulder with kisses. I roll onto my back so I can face him.

"Good morning," I say in an overly sleepy voice.

"Hey," he says as he pushes strands of hair from my face.

"How did you sleep?" he asks.

"I didn't," I say. "I had this amazing guy talk to me and cuddle me all night."

"Oh, you poor girl," he says with a pouty lip.

I pull him into me and wrap both my arms around him. "As much as I want to do this all morning, I have to get home. Kadin has a soccer game today that I promised her I'd go to."

"I'll drive you on my way to the gym. We have a morning workout."

"Do you mind if I shower?" I ask.

"Can I join you?" he says with the guiltiest smirk I've ever seen.

"Next time?" It's a question because nothing sexual happened last night after Jett and Hayes interrupted us, and now, looking back, I'm really glad they did. I'm not sure; after a short couple of months, I'm ready to have sex with Tate. I'm not even sure how I feel about him other than he has a sexy body, and that's no reason to have sex with him. Or is it? Oh, gosh, I need my mom.

After I shower and find all my clothes, I make my way from his bedroom to God knows what will be waiting for me on the other side of that door. I have no idea where Jett ended up last night, and I'm a little fearful he took a girl home to my room to get back at me for kicking him out of his room. That thought makes me chuckle as I make my way into the living room. Walking down the long hallway of door after door, my imagination gets the best of me. How many different girls ended up behind those doors nightly? This thought makes me so happy. Although I was one of them last night, I didn't have sex in one of those rooms.

Walking into the living area, I'm shocked to find a few guys sitting around their breakfast table and the smell of fresh coffee. I don't know why I thought I'd walk out to beer bottles littering the coffee table, red solo cups strewn across the carpet, the stench of vomit filling the air, but nope, just a few guys and their coffee.

Tate walks up behind me, wraps his arms around my waist, and walks me to the kitchen where the guys are. My cheeks flush when they all look up at us.

"Good morning," I say just over a whisper and wave as if

I'm in a parade.

They all give me a friendly nod. I'm assuming the walk of shame is nothing new to these guys, and since Tate is Tate, there's no chance I'm not the first girl to emerge from his bedroom after a winning game. How do I tell them all? *'Nothing happened. I'm not just another trophy?'*

"I'm going to drive Hazel home, then head to the gym," Tate says, already heading for the door. "I'll meet y'all there in an hour. Be ready to work. We have a lot to do before the playoffs."

That sets all the guys into motion, with them rising from the table and scrambling off to get ready for their morning workout routine.

"Demanding," I say with a grin as I look up at him, still standing behind me, my back pushed against his front.

"You should see me on the field," he whispers into my ear, sending a sensation down my body that makes me regret not doing more than just sleeping next to him last night.

• • •

Walking into our house is a stark contrast to the house I just left. There's no smells of fresh coffee brewing, no football boys lounging at the breakfast table, and no Tate wrapping me up in his tight, warm embrace. Just the quiet of the early morning where no one has ventured from the comfort of their bed. Quietly, I cross to Kadin's room, and the floor creaks below me.

"Welcome home," a deep, sleepy voice comes from the couch.

I jump. "Hayes, you scared the shit out of me," I whisper shout, trying not to wake anyone else up. "What are you doing on the couch?"

He sits up, and his disheveled blond hair appears over the back of the couch. "I slept here. I tried to wait up for you, but you never came home."

Confused, I ask, "Why? you have a bedroom." I make my way to his makeshift bed and sit beside him.

"Because I promised your parents I'd take care of you three years ago when they dropped us off."

"Hayes, you know it's not the first time I've stayed out all night." I mean I don't make a habit of it but he's never cared before.

"I know it's the first time you stayed out without one of us with you," he says as he rubs his chin.

I try to remember the other times I've stayed out all night, and maybe he's right. Maybe one of the girls stayed with me, or at the very least, Jett.

"And that's your only reason for staying up? Because you promised my mom years ago to babysit me. Not because you were jealous I spent the night with another boy last night?" I say, nudging him with a teasing grin.

"Boy is right because Tate is not a man."

"So, you are jealous," I retort as I lay my head on his lap and look at him. "Not to sound repetitive, but you don't have to babysit me. My parents don't expect you to watch me. Maybe when I was eighteen, but we're not kids anymore, Hayes. I'm not the girl you used to chase around the playground."

He pulls my hair into a makeshift ponytail on top of my head and says, "It's early in California; don't make me call your parents."

I roll my eyes and try to change the subject because I don't want to talk to my parents and break down the events of last night because God knows my mom will ask. And ask. And ask until I tell her every inappropriate detail.

"Where did Jett stay last night?" I ask, still lying on his lap, closing my eyes as he plays with my hair.

"My room. He's upstairs still."

"With a girl?"

"Do you think I'd be on the couch and give up my bed if he wasn't?"

"Well, at least someone is having sex in your bed," I joke, covering my face just before he takes all my hair that he has in his hand and whips me with it.

"Ouch!" I exclaim.

He covers my mouth and shushes me. "Let's enjoy the quiet before everyone is up and running."

"Does Olivia know Jett was with a girl last night?" I ask, tilting my head slightly to look up at Hayes.

"Yeah, I think so," he replies, his fingers still moving gently through my hair. He pauses for a minute, and I can feel a shift in his demeanor. "Have you noticed she's been…different lately? She's been skipping classes and not coming out with us as much."

I nod, biting my lip. "I've noticed. I thought maybe it was just school stress, but something has felt off for a while. I guess I've been trying to ignore it."

"Yeah," he says, his voice quieter now. "I've been worried about her. She hasn't. been herself lately." He trails off, his hand stilling in my hair for a moment, like he's lost in thought.

The tension in the air is growing. I shift a little, trying to change the subject. "Does Kadin know about Jett?" I ask, hoping to make things a little less intense. But I make a mental note to check in on Olivia to see what's been bothering her.

"Kadin?" he asks, surprised.

"Come on…don't play dumb; you know she's been in love with Jett since the first day in kindergarten."

He blinks down at me, his expression twisting with disbelief. "Seriously!" he says, his eyes widening as he leans back slightly, the disbelief clear in his tone. His mouth hangs open for a second before he shakes his head, clearly trying to process what I just said.

I shift slightly, still lying on Hayes's lap. "Do you know why Jett and Olivia broke up when we went home for the summer? I mean they dated most of our junior year."

Hayes nods, his brow furrowing slightly. "Yeah, I remember. Olivia said something about it being too weird with their families around."

"Do you believe her?" I say, looking up at him. "She said it was awkward being together around our families, and then they just kind of drifted, but what if she felt guilty about Kadin?"

"I don't know, Hazel, nor is it any of my business. But, I do know they're back to hooking up?" Hayes asks, his fingers pausing for a moment before continuing to play with my hair.

"Yep. On and off! I see Jett sneaking out of her room to yours all the time."

Hayes smirks. "Figures."

I roll my eyes. "Honestly, I'd rather they keep sneaking around. It's less awkward when they're not official."

Hayes laughs softly. "Yeah, because when they're official, it's like the whole world has to know."

"Exactly!" I laugh too, but then my smile fades. "It's got to be killing Kadin, though. She'd never admit it, but seeing them together has to hurt."

I glance up at Hayes, his fingers still running through my hair, and I can't help but think about how things used to be. Back in high school, he took up so much space in my head, and I was sure there was no one else like him. We were inseparable, and everyone always assumed we were more than just friends. And maybe, for a long time, I wanted that too. I was addicted to him—his presence, his laugh, the way he'd look at me like I was the only one in the room.

But that was then.

Now, lying here with him, it feels…different. I'm not the same girl who used to get butterflies just because he walked into a room. We've both changed. Sure, there's still a connection, something that's always been there between us, but it's not as intense anymore. Not the way it was in high school.

"What are you thinking about?"

His smooth voice jolts me out of my daydream.

"Just how happy I am that we're friends," I say as I look into his eyes, and he runs his fingertip along the shape of my face.

"Do you like him?" Hayes asks, still exploring all the surfaces of my face.

"Who? Tate?" I ask.

"Yes, who else?" He shakes his head.

"I do," I answer honestly. "It's only been a few months, but I do really like him. He makes me feel special, and I think he really likes me too."

"Are you going to introduce him to your parents?" Hayes asks.

I pause for a minute, shaking my head as I answer. "No, not yet. You and Jett are the only boys who have ever met my parents, and I'm okay keeping it that way."

Hayes leans down, kisses my forehead, and says, "So am I."

And just like that, the love-sick girl from high school is back, wishing he was kissing me on more places than just my forehead.

I jump up and straddle him, and before he can throw me off, I say, "It won't be like this forever. One day, some guy is going to sweep me off my feet, and my parents will fall madly in love with him, and you, Jett, Kadin, and Olivia will all have to make room for him because he'll be my person, and we'll have a million babies and live happily ever after."

"What if you already met him?" he asks, his voice soft but steady, his eyes locked onto mine like he's searching for something deep inside me, something unspoken. I can feel his gaze pulling at me, and for a minute, it's as if the world narrows to just the two of us.

"Tate?" I mutter, the name slipping out almost absentmindedly. "My happily ever after isn't Tate," I say, my voice firmer, but the way Hayes is looking at me makes the word feel shaky.

His lips twitch, and his breath is warm against my skin as he leans in closer. "What if I didn't mean Tate?" he whispers.

The air between us seems to thicken, and I press my forehead against his, so close that my vision blurs, my eyes crossing. It's disorienting like I've put my contacts in the wrong eyes, but I don't pull away. I can feel his breath mixing with mine, the tension between us so tangible it's hard to breathe.

"You're being very weird right now, Hayes Emmerson. Are you still drunk from last night?"

Just then, someone clears their throat to get our attention. I spring up to my feet out of instinct, breaking free from the hold Hayes has on me.

"Didn't you get enough last night?" Jett questions.

Hayes and I both point at each other.

"Hayes is being very weird," I fumble to tell Jett with way too much inflection in my voice. "What did you give him last night? I think he's still on it, whatever it was."

Jett's forehead wrinkles as he lifts his eyebrows, his nose scrunching like he's just smelled something foul.

"What look is that?" Hayes questions.

"Yeah, why do you look so weird right now?" I add.

Jett shakes his head and puts his hands together in front of his chest. "Listen, you two, don't try to deflect right now. You all look really guilty right now, and Tate is—"

I interrupt him before he can finish his sentence. "Stop it. It's Hayes. Nothing weird is happening. We were talking and started to joke around." I'm babbling right now, but I continue with my frenzied explanation, praying he believes me.

"I literally just spent the night with Tate and got dropped off less than an hour ago. What could be happening here?"

From my peripherals, I can see Hayes sink into himself a little, and it gives me the strangest feeling in my stomach. Jett covers his ears.

Looking between the two of them, I say, "What? You asked."

Then, in unison, they chorus, "No, Hazel, we didn't ask."

I shrug and walk into my bedroom.

# Chapter 7

## HAYES

Watching Hazel leave the room, I sink back onto the couch.

"What the fuck was that?" Jett asks as he sits down next to me.

I push my hand through my hair and answer, "I have no idea, man. What is wrong with me?"

"What do you mean?"

"I mean, I can't stop obsessing over Hazel lately," I snap back.

Putting his hands over his ears like a toddler trying to avoid discipline, he sings, "Lalalalalala."

"Stop!" I shove his hands from his ears. "I'm being serious right now."

"Hayes, I don't want to know this. I don't want to have to keep a secret from Hazel and the girls or my team captain. Maybe you're just jealous? I mean, it's not often that Hazel dates, and we both know she's only had eyes for you for years. Now that she's not at your beck and call, you finally see her. But come on, man, don't fuck this up for her. Tate likes her, he's popular, and she's having a really good time for the first time in a long time."

"What do you mean?"

Jett lays his head against the back of the couch and moans. "Hayes, she's been chasing you for years, never going out with guys watching you fuck anyone you wanted to. Never allowing her feelings to affect our friend group."

"Why didn't anyone tell me?"

"Hayes, you knew," Jett says as he puts his hand on my knee to lift himself off the couch. "I have to go, man. I have to get to practice with the guys. I'll see you all later.

"Hey, is there a girl still in my room?" I ask as he walks away as if it were an everyday occurrence.

He looks over his shoulder and smiles, which is all I need to answer my question.

"Can you take her with you?" I ask before he closes the door.

"Sorry, man, I'm late. I have to go." And just like that, Jett rushes out of the door.

I quietly knock on Kadin's door, trying to avoid Hazel since things are all in my head right now.

"Come in," Kadin moans, and I can tell her head is buried in her pillow.

Peeking my head in, I say, "I need your help."

"It's too early," she groans.

"Come on, Kadin. I slept on the couch last night waiting for Hazel."

She pops up like a whack-a-mole. "What do you mean? Hazel never came home last night?"

"No," I say. "Some friend you are!" She could've gotten herself in trouble."

"She's always in trouble, Hayes. Where have you been the last seven years of our friendship?" she hisses.

"More like ten years," I argue.

"Hayes, it's too early for this. What do you want?"

"Huh?" I question.

Kadin moves her arm in front of her from one side to the other and says, "Why are you in my room so early?"

"Oh yeah, sorry. There's a girl in my room that Jett left there. Can you get her out?"

She tilts her head to the left and says, "You know that's a Hazel job, not a Kadin job. I don't do confrontation; I do fun and life of the party. Hazel does confrontation and loves it. Go ask her to do it?"

"No."

"Eww, don't snap at me. Why can't she help?"

"Has anyone ever told you that you ask too many questions?" I ask, frustration overcoming me at this point.

She crosses her arms, and it's hard to miss that she's not wearing a bra, but I do my best to look straight into her eyes, letting her know I mean business.

"Has anyone ever told you that you get more bees with honey than…" Her voice trails off. She looks to the sky, perhaps hoping the rest of the riddle is up there somewhere, and then she looks back to me for help.

I press my lips together into a thin line, then say, "Don't look at me. I have no idea what you're trying to say."

"What I'm trying to say is don't be a dick, and maybe I'll help you." She huffs.

"Oh, okay, yeah, you should've just said that. I'm not asking you to be mean to the girl; I'm asking you to get her out of my room so I can sleep and shower."

"Ugh," Kadin moans as she slides off her bed, walks over to me, and grabs me by my wrists to drag me down the hall to my room. She quickly knocks on my door, like how I knocked on hers, but there is nothing. Kadin looks at me and then to the door again and whispers, "I hate you, Hayes."

She opens the door and peeks her head in as if there's a wild animal about to jump out at us. Under my blankets, a mound and a ton of brown hair spills over my pillowcase.

Kadin looks back at me, a playful smirk tugging at her lips. She raises an eyebrow and asks, "Are you sure you don't want to just get into bed with her? She was probably thinking you brought her here last night; she was so drunk last night; she wouldn't know the difference." Her eyes sparkle with mischief as she gives me a teasing nudge, clearly enjoying the chance to make fun of me.

I consider this thought process for a minute, and it's not a terrible idea. Just then, a whisper behind us scares the crap out of me.

"What are you doing?"

I jump and fall into Hazel, who just snuck up behind me.

"Hazel, what the fuck? You scared the crap out of me."

Before she can answer, Kadin sighs and says, "Thank God you're here. There's a girl in there," she says, pointing at the door. "And Hayes needs her gone."

Hazel's head tilts slightly, her lips parting as if she's not sure what to say. She hesitates for a minute before speaking. "You have a girl here?" she asks, her voice laced with confusion, but there's something else – a sharpness I've never heard before, and her posture stiffens like she's bracing for something.

*Is she…jealous?*

I quickly shake the thought away; she's with Tate, of course, she's not jealous. "No! It's Jett's date from last night. Seriously, Hazel, I was sleeping on the couch waiting for you to get home."

She gives me a slow, deliberate once-over, crossing her arms over her chest, and again, it's impossible not to notice she's not wearing a bra either. Her chest is small, but perfect, a small B-cup – more than enough to grab my attention. Hazel's eyes lock onto mine, sharp and intense, like she's searching for something, but all I can do is stare back.

She's standing there, maybe five-foot-three inches, short enough that I have to glance down to meet her gaze. Her head shakes slightly when she catches me gawking at her, like she's annoyed or maybe just confused by the way I can't seem to look away.

"Something you like?" she asks, her voice teasing, but there's an edge to it, too.

And it's at that moment I realize she realizes I'm still staring at her tits.

I clear my throat and say, "Listen, I know that neither of you girls has a bra on right now, and it's really unfair. Can we make a rule that bras must be worn at all times outside of the privacy of your bedroom?"

In unison, they shout, "Absolutely not!"

And Hazel, being Hazel, adds, "Hayes, you'll move out before I agree to that rule." She slaps my dick while making her way past me into my bedroom.

I fall over in agony as I watch her pull the blankets from the top of my bed onto the floor. There lays a half-naked college girl I've never seen and probably will never see again. She scurries to the top of my bed, trying to hide herself, and Hazel bends down, grabs her clothes, and tosses them at her.

"Hey, I'm Hazel," she says, her voice casual but with a hint of authority. She gestures to Kadin, adding, "And this is Kadin," before pointing to me. "And that's Hayes. You're in his room, but the way."

She pauses for effect, her eyes narrowing slightly. "I'd highly recommend leaving in the next five minutes unless you're interested in sharing a bed with this guy and I wouldn't suggest that."

"What the fuck, Hazel?" I ask.

She shrugs, grabs my hand, and helps me from my knees. Once standing, I tower over her, but she doesn't care. She takes my hands and places them on each of her boobs.

She stands on her toes and whispers, "You've seen them, and you've touched them; move on, Hayes, they're just boobs." And she walks away.

Kadin and I both look at each other.

"What just happened?" Kadin asks, and I can only shrug with saucers for eyes.

Because what the fuck did just happen? And why did I touch Hazel Jones' boobs in our hallway with two other girls watching? And why did I find it so hot? Hazel and I have had sex a few times before, usually when we've both been drinking. Inhibitions are low, and there is no fear of feeling too much, but it's never been like that for me. I remember every encounter vividly—every sound she makes, every ticklish spot on her body, what she likes and dislikes. I know she has a birthmark on her right side, right at the curve of her waist, and a group of freckles on the inner part of her left arm that resemble stars on a clear Texas night. I remember how I felt inside her. It's a feeling that repeats over and over.

# Chapter 8

## JETT



Senior Year

Five...four...three...two...one...

The stadium erupts!

I can hear the roar of the crowd, but they do not trump the cheers of my teammates.

What a way to finish the first half of my final year at college. We're finally seniors and only have a few months left of college. I watch as all the students rush to the field, and it's complete and utter chaos like I've never seen before. I grew up near LA in California, so concerts, sporting events, and just mass amounts of people congregating are not a new concept to me. Crowds are typical in LA, but this...this is special. This is love, love for one's school, love for one's football team, and love for one's fellow teammates and classmates. This is everyone banded together by the name on the front of our shirts, being a part of something bigger than us. And it's a feeling I'll never forget.

"We did it!" I scream to nobody, my voice getting lost in

the cool November night air. My breath swirls in front of me as the crisp Texas night wraps around me, but the adrenaline coursing through my veins keeps me warm. I punch the air with my right hand, holding my helmet in my left. "We did it!" I yell again, exhilaration bursting from every pore as the victory sinks in.

Everything feels sharper and more vivid. I've never felt more alive than I do at this moment. The vibrant colors of the field, the bright lights, and the scoreboard – the one that's broken my heart so many times before tonight.

Josh, one of our linebackers, picks me up and carries me over his shoulder to the fifty-yard line. He sets me down, and I'm immediately flooded with an overwhelming sense of pride and accomplishment. All the hard work, practice, and dedication have paid off, and it's an incredibly validating experience. The struggle, the sweat, the moments of doubt—all of it was worth it for this moment of triumph.

"Jett...Jett..."

I hear Olivia shouting my name from a few feet away, but the crowds of people are making it impossible to get to her. I see Hazel break off and maneuver her way to get to Tate.

A slap on my pad grabs my attention. Hayes stands there, ready to congratulate me.

"Awesome game," he shouts in my ear.

"I'm so proud of you," he continues, not allowing me to talk. "You did so good tonight. I wish your parents were here to see you play. You look amazing, bud."

I hug him and say, "Thanks, man, I could've never gotten here without you; you know that, right."

"Hey, I gotta go, but I couldn't leave without congratulating you." He pauses and looks around. "Have you seen Hazel?"

"Yeah, she's with Tate." I motion in their direction with my head. "I'll see you tonight, right?"

"Of course," he mutters as he turns to walk away.

I watch his head dip just the faintest bit. No one but me would notice the subtle drop, and the ping of guilt I feel is real.

Hayes was always a better football player than me. He's faster and just has a better mind for the game. He can read a play before it happens, and there are not many players who have the ability to do that.

I was on the sideline the day he got hit in our senior year. I'll never forget the sound when everything in his shoulder tore. I felt it when he hit the thirty-yard line. Our coaches tried to keep me from running out there to him, but they couldn't stop me. He begged me not to remove his helmet because he didn't want anyone to see him cry. I knelt over him for what felt like an eternity, waiting for the ambulance, and cried with him while I held his hand. We've never told anyone that story.

I thought football would come between us once he couldn't play, but he's been my number-one fan. He's the best coach I could ever ask for, and I know I'd never be here standing on this field today without him.

"I'm so proud of you!"

I'm pulled from my thoughts as my one and only wraps her arms around me.

"Olivia!" I pick her up and swing her around like we're in some cheesy movie.

"I can't believe it! What a way to finish your college career," she says, and before I can respond, she kisses me like no one else is around. I melt into her, letting the moment swallow me whole, her taste better than tonight's win.

Then I hear it – a throat clearing beside us. I crack open one eye, lips still locked on Olivia, and see Kadin standing there. My best friend, the one who's been with me through everything. But right now, the look in her eyes isn't what I expected. There's something off – disappointment? Hurt?

"Hello, you two, I'm here," she says, her voiced forced, too cheerful.

Guilt twists in my gut, and I untangle myself from Olivia. I try to bring Kadin into our moment, pulling her into a hug with both of us, but the energy feels wrong. We start jumping up and down, yelling, but the usual joy is missing. The look on her face lingers in my mind, even as we celebrate.

# Chapter 9

## HAZEL



Senior Year

I get hit in my side, and before I can scream at whoever is trying to separate me from the girls, I'm hoisted up in the air by Tate, and the rush makes my head spin. I slide down his sweaty body, and he wraps his arms around me.

"We won!" Tate shouts. "We did it!"

"I know; I'm so proud of you; you were freaking awesome out there tonight," I yell back in his ear.

He kisses me, and there are flashes from cameras all around us. I'm not shy, but this is overwhelming.

I yell in his ear, "I hope our parents don't see this."

"I do," he says as he wraps me up in another tight, hot, sweaty kiss.

We've been dating for several months now, but I still haven't told my parents about him. I don't keep secrets from them, but this is different. I like Tate a lot, and if I'm honest with my parents, then they'll want to meet him, and whatever is happening between him and me will become real, and I'm not sure if I'm ready for anything real outside the real feelings I have for Hayes.

When I went home for the summer like I always do, Tate stayed back in Texas with his family and for football, so there wasn't really a reason to tell my parents. But now, with Tate here and Hayes always lingering at the edges of my thoughts, it feels like I'm walking a tightrope. Every time I'm with Tate, I can't help but wonder what it would be like with Hayes. The what-ifs circle in my mind – what if we stopped dancing around each other? What is there's more between us than we're willing to admit? Being caught between them makes it impossible to ignore the pull Hayes has always had on me, no matter how much I try.

The roar of Tate's name snaps me out of my head. His name being yelled at us from all directions: students, parents, alumni, and reporters. It's absolute mayhem. I yell at him again because that's all I can do—yell because a normal volume isn't an option right now.

"Do what you need to do. I'll wait over here with the girls. You have fans that need you." I motion in the direction of the girls with my head.

"No, don't leave. I want you here with me for this," he says.

"Are you sure?" I ask, feeling really uncomfortable in the crowd. "I feel like I'm just in the way; I feel like they don't want me here," I whisper shout into his ear.

He pulls me in tighter to his side, not allowing any distance to come between us. I look around to make sure I can still see my friends, and they're still here, just a few feet away, celebrating with Jett.

My phone vibrates in my pocket, and without even looking at the caller ID, I hit accept, assuming it's Hayes looking for us on the field.

"Hello," I shout into my phone, pressing it to my ear. I know all my makeup will be on the screen by the time this call is over. I cover my other ear as I try to listen to the person on the phone.

"Hazel, it's Mom."

Completely forgetting I'm two hours ahead of my parents, I ask, "Why are you calling so late? Is everything okay?"

"I'm watching you on TV."

"What?" I yell into the phone. "Mom, I can't hear you. We're on the field. We just won the championships. I have to call you later."

"You're on TV with a super cute boy," she blurts out before I can hang up the phone. "Who's the boy holding you tighter than the trophy he just won?"

I'm silent.

"Hazel, are you there?"

"Um, yeah, Mom, I have to go. I'll be home in a few weeks for winter break. We'll talk then." I quickly hang up and get a very uneasy feeling in my stomach, and I can't rationalize why. If I were on TV with Jett and the girls, this wouldn't be weird at all. We'd all be celebrating and waving at the cameras, but with Tate, I'm just here. Not talking, not yelling, not celebrating. Just standing here like an awkward human-sized trophy while my friends are bouncing off the walls celebrating together steps away from me, and I've never felt so left out.

Tate is pulled away to talk to a reporter, so I take this opportunity to rejoin my friends. I rush over and jump on Jett's back. He looks up and sees it's me, and we all start jumping up and down again and enjoy our own private mosh pit.

"Where's Hayes?" I yell into Jett's ear.

"I don't know," he says with a shrug.

Kadin must have overheard me from underneath Jett's arms,

her shoulders currently bearing most of Jett's body weight, as she says, "I saw him for a minute earlier, and then he just disappeared."

The celebration feels wrong somehow, like something's missing. The crowd is cheering, everyone's jumping up and down, but all I can think about is how strange it feels that Hayes isn't here. He should be. He's always been here, right by our sides, through every win, every loss, always the one cheering the loudest for Jett.

But tonight, without him, the energy feels incomplete, like a puzzle with one missing piece. I hate that I can't stop thinking about it, especially because Tate is right here beside me. Tate, my boyfriend. The one I should be celebrating with, the one I should be focused on. But instead, my mind keeps wandering back to Hayes, to how things feel off without him.

It's not fair. Tate deserves all of my attention, all of my excitement, but something about this night makes it impossible to ignore the fact that maybe things are changing. That maybe we're not those same kids who grew up together, inseparable, always knowing our place in each other's lives.

• • •

The cool night air doesn't do much to ease the tension swirling around us as we stand outside the locker room, waiting. Kadin is unusually quiet, arms crossed tightly over her chest, her eyes darting between the locker room doors and Olivia, who seems tired, almost worn down. Olivia rubs her forehead, her face pale in the harsh stadium lights. It's obvious she's struggling, though—her usual liveliness dimmed, and yet she doesn't say anything. Maybe she doesn't care, or maybe she's just too tired to notice the tension between her and Kadin.

We've been waiting forever, and the silence between Kadin and Olivia is thick. I shift on my feet, glancing between them, unsure if I should say something to break the tension. But I can't shake the unease in my own chest, and it's not just from them.

"So…are we just going to stand here pretending we're not all miserable, or are we actually going to talk about whatever's going on?" I blurt out, crossing my arms to mirror Kadin's stance.

Kadin shoots me a look, her jaw tightening. "We are you talking about, Hazel?"

I shrug, trying to play it cool, but the tension thickens even more. "I don't know, maybe the fact that you two are acting like strangers all of a sudden." I glance at Olivia, who offers nothing but a tired sigh.

I throw my hands up in mock surrender. "All right, good talk," I say.

The silence returns, but now it feels worse, and I can't help but think I've made things even more awkward. As usual.

I try to focus on the locker room doors, willing Tate and Jett to come out already, but it doesn't stop my mind from wandering back to Hayes. How am I supposed to fully love Tate when a part of me still can't let go of Hayes?

Finally, the creak of the locker room doors pulls me from my thoughts, and I look up. Tate and Jett are walking toward us, laughing together, completely oblivious to the tension they're about to step into. Relief washes over me that the waiting is over, but it's quickly overshadowed by the confusion still tugging at my heart.

We pile into the Uber, squeezing in awkwardly. Kadin slides in last, her expression tight, avoiding eye contact with anyone. The car is quiet, aside from the driver's radio softly playing in the background. I glance at Kadin, trying to catch her eye, but she stares out of the window, arms crossed.

When the car pulls up to the bar, packed with people spilling out of the doorways and windows, Olivia sighs. "I think I'm going to head home. I'm not feeling great," she says quietly, her voice tired.

I glance over and see it—she's exhausted, her face pale, and she's been fading all night. Before I can even respond, Jett is already moving. "I'll go with you," he says, leaning over to touch her am.

Kadin throws her hands up. "You know what? I think I'll meet up with some other friends. You guys go ahead." Her tone is casual, but I feel the sting of her words.

She doesn't even wait for a response before stepping out of the car and taking off across the street to a different bar.

My heart sinks. We always go together. But lately, things have been off, and this just feels like more proof that everything's changing.

I turn to Tate beside me, who seems oblivious, already scanning the crowd outside the bar like he's ready for a good time. I wish I could push the hurt away, but I can't.

"We should head inside," Tate says as he steps out of the Uber, holding his hand out to me.

I follow him out, but before taking his hand, I lean down to look into the car. "Text me when you get home," I tell Olivia, my voice soft.

The car pulls away, and the heaviness in my chest tightens as I watch them disappear into the night.

My eyes shift across the street to the bar that Kadin walked into alone. Everything feels different now, fractured somehow. I glance at Tate, who's still waiting for me, his smile carefree. He nudges me gently, pulling me back into the moment.

"Come on," he says with a grin. "Let's just enjoy the night."

I force a small smile and nod, taking his hand as we approach the bar. The sound of laughter and muffled music grows louder as we approach the bar entrance. Tate pulls open the door, the smell of stale beer and the warmth from inside washing over me. The lighting is dim, and the space is crowded.

"What do you want to drink?" Tate yells at me.

"Whatever is fastest. I'll go look for a table or something; just call my cell if you can't find me."

That's how packed it is in here. I know there is zero chance of scoring a table, but I'm not a quitter. Scanning the entire bar for a table, I see Hayes back in the corner with a few of the guys from the team.

I jump up and down, yelling, "Hayes!" but he can't hear me. I make myself as skinny as possible and work my way down the long hallway to the back of the bar. When I finally make it and approach the group, Hayes's back is to me. With a mischievous grin, I sneak up behind him, and cover his eyes with my hands.

"Guess who?" I shout.

In slow motion, he reaches behind him and pulls me into him. His hand wraps around my waist, sending a familiar jolt of electricity through me, and instinctively, I pull away slightly, remove my hands, and shout, "Hey, you can't grope me like that!" I protest, my voice light and full of surprise. "Where were you tonight when we all rushed the field?"

"Too many people for me," he shouts over the roar of the bar into my ear.

"And this isn't." I motion to the chaos surrounding us.

"I can drink here." He raises his beer just as Tate walks over and clicks his beer to Hayes.

"Good game tonight," Hayes congratulates Tate, but it's not

sincere; nothing about what is happening right now between the two of them is friendly.

"Thanks," Tate replies, his tone guarded.

The air is feeling even more cramped than it was five minutes ago, thick with unsaid words and unspoken challenges. Tate doesn't avoid Hayes's gaze as he grabs me, pulls me into him, and kisses me, claiming me. A mix of beer and tequila from his lips fills my senses. Hayes's eyes are on him, probing, searching for weakness.

Trying to break through the tension, I ask Tate, "How much did you have to drink from the bar to here?" I move my tongue over my teeth and through my mouth, tasting the different alcohol his kiss has left behind.

"Everyone was buying me shots; it would be rude to turn them down."

I nod and say, "There was nowhere to sit, so I figured you'd want to hang with your friends."

"How lucky that we found your friend too, isn't that right, Hayes?" Tate says, raising his voice slightly to cut through the noise.

Hayes responds by putting a hand to his ear, pretending he can't hear, a smirk tugging at his lips. The usual tension between them simmers just beneath the surface, and I already feel my energy draining.

I should be excited to be here, but I'm not. Kadin's decision to ditch us for her other friends is still nagging at me. I can't shake the worry I feel for Olivia either, the way she looked so pale and exhausted earlier. And the last thing I want tonight is to stand here and watch Tate and Hayes try to outdo each other, as if I'm some prize to be won. I'm really not in the mood for any of this.

"Hey, Tate," I say, tapping his arm. "I'm super tired, but I don't want to pull you away since we just got here. I'm going to take an Uber home. We'll catch up tomorrow."

"No," he drags out the 'O' for effect. "Don't leave me, baby."

*Baby,* I think to myself. No one calls me baby; that's cringe.

Totally unphased by the repulsed look that's no doubt on my face, he continues, "Baby, stay with me tonight. We need to celebrate my championship." He waggles his eyebrows, and that's it. I'm out of here.

"Nah, I'm good; I need to check on Olivia. She wasn't feeling well today."

"You sure?"

"Yes, I'm sure," I yell back at him as I stand on my tippy toes and kiss him quickly on his lips.

I make my way from the bar entrance onto the sidewalk and let the fresh air invade my lungs.

"Hazel, wait up," I hear Hayes shout behind me.

Looking back, I ask, "What's up?"

"Nothing. I'll ride home with you."

"You didn't have to leave; I'll make it home just fine."

"I know; I'm not in the mood to party tonight. I'd rather hang out with you."

I put my hand on his forehead like a mother would to her sick child and say, "Hayes, are you feeling okay? Do you have a fever? Do you need a doctor?"

This causes him to chuckle, and he shoves me off the curb into the street, never letting go of my oversized jersey that reads Baker on the back.

I get into the Uber before Hayes, and he says, "Take that jersey off, Hazel."

"Why?" I ask as I scrunch my face up and look at him over my shoulder.

"I'm not getting in an Uber with you while you're wearing

another guy's name on your back that doesn't belong there in the first place."

"He's my boyfriend, Hayes."

"Keep telling yourself that, Hazel."

"What does that mean?" I say, growing irritated with his innuendo.

"Nothing. Can we grab food on the way home? I'm starving."

"Can we just grab Olivia and Jett something, too? I wasn't lying back there when I said I wanted to check on Olivia. She and Jett went straight home after the game. She's been missing a lot of school lately, and I'm a little worried about her."

"Sure, but you know, Hazel, you worry too much. You're going to end up like your mom." He pulls me closer to him in the backseat of our Uber.

"Is that such a bad thing?" I say, looking up at him.

"No, you know I've always had a thing for your mom."

"Ew, gross!" I shout, pushing myself away from him.

# Chapter 10

## HAZEL

Hayes and I quietly enter our house and set the food on the coffee table. I walk over to Olivia's door and hesitantly put my ear to the door to see if she's awake.

"Creeper," Hayes whisper shouts from the living room, and I flip him off.

Jett and Olivia are talking, so I quietly knock. "Hey, it's me. You guys decent?"

"Yes, come in," Olivia's voice comes from the other side of the door.

"We got food if you guys are hungry."

"Who's we?' Jett asks.

"Hayes and I. Who else?"

"Um, I don't know, Hazel. Maybe your boyfriend," Jett says with a tinge of snark in his voice.

Pretending his tone doesn't affect me, I say, "Oh, he's drunk at the bar, and I'm here. Hayes and I shared an Uber because you know he lives here," I say, giving him a little bit of his snark back. "Anyway, are you hungry?"

Jett kisses Olivia on the forehead and walks past me to the

living room where Hayes is, and I know by the time I get out there, all the food will be gone.

"How do you feel?" I ask, sitting on her bed and folding my legs crisscross applesauce.

"I'm okay; I just got a little overwhelmed at the football game."

"Olivia, you've missed like twenty days of school the past two months. You're going to get dropped. You need to go to the doctor."

"I have an appointment on Monday at 8 a.m. Would you be willing to skip class and go with me?" Olivia asks, her voice steady, but there's a crack in her casual façade. She plays with the blankets, avoiding my eyes. Olivia has always been the responsible one, the oldest sibling, constantly trying to set an example. But right now, she's not trying to probe anything. There's a flicker of worry in her gaze, a vulnerability she rarely shows, as if asking for help feels like admitting defeat.

"Of course I will. Any excuse to miss school and I'm in. Colonoscopy, I'm down, cliff jumping; count me in. But do you think I can get a doctor's note, too?" I say, joking, and we both laugh.

• • •

Monday morning comes quicker than expected since I spent the entire weekend avoiding Tate. After I left the bar Friday, let's just say the shots didn't stop, and there are several pictures of Tate and a random girl on our campus social media group. He's sent flowers and come by the house at least five times over the weekend, but Hayes has been more than accommodating to run interference for me. When Tate couldn't get past Hayes, he text me.

*Tate* – Hazel, nothing happened. I swear.

*Tate* – She's totally irrelevant.

This text makes me feel even worse if something did happen. We've been together since my junior year, and all it takes is one drunken night, and he cheats on me with some random girl.

*Tate* – Hazel, stop ghosting me.

*Tate* – I'm coming over, and I swear I'm going to beat the shit out of Hayes and his smug smile.

*Me* – Don't come here. I'm not home. You're an asshole. Don't call me again.

*Tate* – That's it? You can't break up with me over some pictures.

*Me* – Yes, that's it. Yes, I can break up with you over some very telling pictures.

*Tate* – Please Hazel

*Me* – Stop. You're making a fool out of yourself, like you did to me Friday night. Just stop, Tate.

If I've learned anything from my parents, it's that the right guy will never put himself in a position to make the right girl doubt him. Tate did that Friday night, and I refuse to settle.

I shove my phone into my purse and look around the

small sterile waiting room. Slow eighties rock echoes quietly through the air, doing little to ease the tension that's settled in my stomach. I watch Olivia as she aimlessly flips through a gossip magazine, clearly trying to distract herself, avoiding conversation.

The door that leads to the examination rooms opens, and the nurse calls Olivia's name. She sighs, closing the magazine with a sharp snap. I stand, shoving my purse under my arm, and follow her down the narrow hallway to the fourth room on the left. The fluorescent light flickers slightly overhead, adding to the sterile atmosphere. I can't help but feel the weight of what's coming, even if Olivia is pretending it's just another appointment.

"You scared?"

"Nope," she says, propping herself onto the examination table.

"How do you feel today?" I ask, handing her a different gossip magazine this time.

"Fine." Again, not looking up.

The doctor walks in, interrupting my interrogation. Olivia sets her magazine down, and I sit up straight. Her doctor looks between the two of us and asks Olivia, "Can we speak freely in front of your friend?"

"I'm her cousin," I interject.

Her doctor looks at me unamused and turns back to Olivia, waiting for permission.

"Oh yeah, she's good, we're good, or I mean… Yes, doctor, you can talk in front of Hazel." She stumbles on every word, trying to get that out while clearly trying to convince me she's not nervous.

"Your urine test shows you're pregnant."

"*Pregnant!*" I interrupt and then place my hand over my

mouth in fear I may get kicked out.

Olivia takes a breath then says, "I'd like to say that's impossible, but clearly, it's not. I'm on the pill, and we use protection, so that leaves like zero-point-zero chance of getting pregnant."

"Then you should probably buy a lottery ticket on the way home, sweetheart," the doctor says, totally unphased by Olivia's shock.

*I dislike this doctor, and if we're having a baby, we need a new one.*

"Wait, so all this sickness… It's because…?" Olivia's words trail off, but I can see the weight of her thoughts swirling behind her eyes. One second she looks relieved, but then it's quickly replaced by something much heavier – uncertainty.

The realization hits me like a wave. She's not sick, not clinically like I feared, but now the possibility of having a baby. What the heck is she going to do with a baby?

"Yes, it seems so. All your symptoms are in line with morning sickness. Although you should know morning sickness in some women doesn't end in the morning. It can go into the afternoon and night. The good news is you should start to feel better in your second trimester. We're going to do a sonogram today to see how far along you are."

The doctor gets out a very long wand and rolls what could be compared to a condom over it.

I look at Olivia and say, "Should I leave?" My eyebrows almost touch my hairline at this point.

"No, come and hold my hand," Olivia insists, her voice soft but determined. She lies on her back, one arm propped under her head. She's wearing one of those flimsy paper gowns that leaves nothing to the imagination.

"Wait," I shout. "Shouldn't we call Jett or FaceTime him?

Will he be mad I'm here, and he's not? Oh My God, I'm freaking out," I say, jumping up and down, trying to control my breath.

Olivia just stares at me with wide eyes, taking in all the humor of this moment. "Hazel, come hold my hand like I asked and let me worry about Jett. There will be plenty of sonograms for him to be a part of. I certainly don't want to share news like this over FaceTime."

Shaking out my hands like I'm readying myself for a marathon. "You're right. That would be a lot to process over the phone. Okay, I'm ready now."

"Will it hurt?" she asks the doctor, searching for reassurance.

"No, not at all."

The room is overcome by a loud, whooshing noise, drowning out the eighties slow rock from earlier. My heart clenches with a mix of fear and love. *Whoosh, whoosh, whoosh*—the sound that can not only be heard but felt in my heart. Tears instantly flow down my face without needing to be told. I know that sound is my best friend's baby.

Being here holding Olivia's hand and listening to her baby's heartbeat echo through this small room has created a bond between us that no one on this earth will ever break. And in this moment, I know nothing will ever replace what Olivia and I share.

# Chapter 11

## OLIVIA

As Hazel drives the car along the familiar route home, the tension is palpable, almost suffocating. The sterile scent of the doctor's office still lingers on me, a reminder of the news that has just rocked my world. Outside, the world rushes by in a blur, oblivious to the seismic shift that just happened to me. Every passing streetlight seems to cast a harsh spotlight on the uncertainty that hangs heavy in the air.

I steal a glance at Hazel beside me, her face a canvas of emotions—shock, disbelief, and perhaps a glimmer of joy amidst the chaos. The weight of the news settles heavily.

"How are you going to tell Jett?"

Hazel's question draws me from my racing thoughts.

"I don't know," I manage, my voice wavering under the weight of uncertainty. It's the only answer I can offer her. Deep down, I know the truth—I'm utterly clueless about how to navigate this situation. How do I tell Jett? He's got his whole future mapped out, dreams of a professional football career shining brightly on the horizon. And a child with me? It was never part of that plan. Fear grips me as I contemplate the revelation that a baby will bring to our lives.

"I can't believe you've been pregnant for twelve weeks and had no idea," Hazel says, trying to fill the silence during the car ride.

"I know it's scary. The irony of being sick is I haven't drunk the entire time I've been pregnant, so at least we're good there."

"I wish I could say the same thing."

I whip my head and look at Hazel.

She holds up her hands and says, "No, not the pregnant part; who wants to be pregnant at our age? No, wait, I didn't mean that. I mean…"

"Just stop," I say. "Put your hands back on the steering wheel. There is precious cargo in the car."

"It's about time you finally admitted your love for me."

We both laugh.

"Speaking of admitting love for you, what is going on with Tate?"

"Absolutely nothing. I'm avoiding him at all costs."

"Does this mean you won't be taking him home with us to meet your parents over winter break?"

"Absolutely not," she says, not taking her eyes off the road. "I'm done. He humiliated me and made me look like a fool with that girl. He's not worth it. I deserve better than that."

"Okay, then what's going on with Hayes?"

"Excuse me!" she says, drawing her eyes to me and not the road.

"Eyes on the road!"

"It's a red light!" she shouts and continues, not giving my request a second thought, "There is nothing going on with Hayes and me." Each of her words is heavy with the weight of her truth, not *the* truth. "Well, I guess that's a lie. The same thing is going on between Hayes and me as it has been since we were kids. He doesn't want to be with me, but he also gets insanely jealous when he sees me with another guy, and I'm tired of it, like physically exhausted."

My eyes search hers, probing for sincerity.

"I've not allowed myself to feel anything for anyone other than Hayes my entire life, and it needs to stop before it destroys my heart. But I can assure you, me breaking up with Tate has nothing to do with Hayes."

"Are you sure? Because you and Hayes have been spending a lot of time together lately."

"Olivia, we live together! Hayes lives with us; of course, we spend a lot of time together." I offer her a nod of acknowledgment before pointing to the light that is now green in front of us.

As Hazel and I walk into the house, Jett and Hayes are lounging on the couch, engrossed in afternoon talk shows. The minute we step inside, Jett's posture shifts. He sits up straighter, his eyes immediately locking onto mine.

"What are you doing here? You should be at school," I say, trying to keep my tone light despite today's events.

Jett stands, crossing the room toward us. "Do you honestly think I could concentrate with you at the doctor's today? What did he say? Did he say anything?" Jett's tone is filled with concern as his eyes volley between mine and Hazel, searching for any sign of reassurance.

The internal monologue I worked on the entire way home has been overtaken by panic.

Hazel rocks back on her heel, excitement emanating from her. She looks to the ceiling, whistling, and I know I can't keep them in suspense any longer.

"Can we talk in my room?" I try to calmly ask, but I'm not sure it worked.

Jett looks from Hazel to me, and without saying anything,

he follows me down the long hallway to my bedroom.

Once he's inside, I quickly shut the door behind him, my heart racing. My palms are slick with sweat, and before I can lose my courage, I blurt out, "I'm pregnant." The sentence feels heavy and final.  I instinctively raise my arms as if to physically brace for his reaction or even embrace the news.

Jett freezes, his body stiffening as if he's just been hit. He blinks, his mouth opening slightly before he shakes his head. "I'm sorry. What did you say?" His voice is quiet, laced with disbelief. "I could've sworn you said you're pregnant, and that's…that's not possible."

Without waiting for me to say 'I'm pregnant' again, Jett is already pacing back and forth in the small area in front of my door. He reminds me of a changed animal looking for a way out.

"Oh no, Olivia, oh no. This can't be happening; we're too young. I have football, oh shit, I have football, Olivia. I'm supposed to go pro. Your parents are going to kill me." Panic takes over his words, and he continues to pace and mumble under his breath.

"Tell me how you're feeling right now?" I plead, trying to get him to articulate his emotions.

"I'm shocked," he says, holding up his index finger. "I'm terrified," he says, holding up a second finger. "I'm so fucking confused," he says, holding up a third finger. "I'm…" He trails off, looking at his hand. "Olivia, you and I break up every time we go home because you say it's weird to be in our hometown together, and the next time we go home, we're going to tell everyone you're pregnant with my child. What is everyone going to think?"

"They're going to think we had unprotected sex," I say matter-of-factly.

"But we didn't!" he shouts as he nervously runs his fingers through his brown hair, ruffling it even more.

Jett glances away for a moment, his cheeks flushed slightly. He bites his lower lip, then scratches the back of his neck, clearly unsure of what to do next. Finally, he reaches out, takes my hand, and leads me to my bed. "Are you okay?" he asks softly, glancing at me through his lashes.

"Yes, I'm okay. I'm scared, but I'm okay."

"Have you thought about what you're going to do?" Jett's innuendo of his question hangs heavy between us.

"What I'm going to do?" I reply, annoyance evident in my tone.

"No, not that," he clarifies, waving his hands from the front of his face. "Like about school and stuff. I assumed you're keeping the baby, right?"

"Yes, of course, I'm keeping this baby." My voice is certain. "I'm twelve weeks pregnant, and I haven't thought about what I will do about school. I'd like to stay here and graduate in May. I'll be the size of a house by then, but I have Hazel, Kadin, and you if you want to be part of this. If not, I'm okay with that as well."

Jett's expression softens. "Olivia, I'm in," he promises. "I'm sorry for my initial reaction. I was caught off guard. We've always been careful, and yet, here we are... *Surprise*! Fate has its own plans for us." He takes my hand and continues, "Listen, we've been friends for fifteen-plus years, and we've been off and on for over a year now. This thing between us isn't a trial run or a 'Let's see how it works out'. This is real. I've wanted to be with you for a long time, and if this speeds things up for us, I'm okay with that."

As his words settle over me, a sense of relief floods my body. I can raise a child with the help of my friends and family but having him excited about our next chapter makes this a dream come true. Jett pulls me onto his lap to straddle him.

Surprised, I whisper, "What are you doing?"

He shrugs and says, "We're alone, and you can't get pregnant."

# Chapter 12

## HAZEL

"What's that about?" Hayes asks, motioning for me to sit next to him.

"It's not my place to say."

"Seriously, Hazel, we're going to play this game?"

"What game? It's not my secret to tell. Maybe you should hear it from Jett."

He leans forward and moves closer to my face, and whispers, "She fucking pregnant, isn't she." Without allowing me to answer, he jumps up and covers his mouth, then squeals like a teenage girl. "Oh my God, Jett is going to flip."

"In a bad way or a good way?" I ask. Completely ashamed that I've just given into him; he guessed right.

"In a good way. Could you imagine anything different from him?"

"No, but you jumped up, and it threw me for a loop."

"I threw you for a loop? Is that a new phrase?"

"I'm an auntie now; I'm broadening my vocabulary," I say, crossing my arms in front of me with defiance.

He moves closer to me and sits back down on the couch.

He pulls me from my cushion and places me on his lap, my legs straddling him.

"What are you doing?" I whisper shout.

"You know what it does to me when you cross your arms, right?"

"Um, no," I answer, completely caught off guard.

"It drives me fucking crazy. It makes me want to take you into my bedroom and fuck the shit out of you."

I try to speak, but all I can get out is a strangled cough. My heart is pounding so hard that I feel as if it's trying to break free. I try to slow it down by breathing more rapidly. But all that does is intensify the feeling that I may die right here.

I clear my throat and say, very calmly I might add, "Um, I'm sorry, but what the fuck did you just say to me?"

"I said I wanted to take you in my room and fuck you. But not like that," Hayes stutters. "I mean like that, but not just that." His hand flies up to rub his face.

My heart pounds as I watch him struggle. He's a mess – tripping over his words, eyes darting between me and the floor, unsure of what to do with himself. And yet, I can't help the shit-eating grin on my face. It's oddly satisfying to see Hayes, who's always so composed, this vulnerable in front of me.

"Hazel," he says, trying to be serious, but I can't wipe the smirk off my face.

I should feel nervous, but instead I feel a twisted sense of power in making him this uncomfortable. The guy who's had me wrapped around his finger for years is unraveling in front of me.

There's no denying that this conversation could go horribly wrong. He could say something that finally pushes me over the edge and breaks us for good, or somehow, this could change everything between us – finally.

He looks at me, his voice is softer now, almost pleading. "Hazel, I'm terrible at this stuff."

"You don't say," I interrupt.

But he ignores my jab and continues. "I have no idea how to do or say anything right when it comes to you. The truth is, I'm a wreck when you're not around. And I can't stand the thought of losing you. You make me feel alive in ways I never thought possible.

"I know I haven't always been the best," he continues, his eyes searching mine for any sign of rejection. "I've screwed up more times than I can count. But through it all, my feelings for you have only gotten stronger. I'm in love with you Hazel. You've always been my girl. I want you to be my girl forever. Can we be Auntie and Uncle H?"

"Seriously?" I laugh, shaking my head. "You say all that, and then you go and ruin it with Auntie and Uncle H."

He grins, that panty-dropping smile that's always disarmed me in the past, and for a second, it almost works. Almost.

"I told you I'm not very good at this," he admits.

I take a deep breath, weighing my options, but the pull toward him is undeniable. My walls are crumbling, and I can't fight it. The truth is, I've wanted this, wanted him, for as long as I can remember. It's terrifying, but it's also exhilarating.

"Lift me off your lap," I say my voice softer now, but filled with intention. "Carry me to my room, and fuck me like you promised."

# Chapter 13

## KADIN

I'll never understand why my college classes are so hard for me to become a middle school P.E. teacher. I'm not teaching math or science; I'm teaching kids the importance of getting outside and moving. It's not like I need to solve complex equations or understand the intricacies of chemical reactions. All I want to do is inspire a love for physical activity and show kids how fun it can be to stay healthy. Yet, here I am, buried under mountains of coursework, struggling to see the relevance of half the material.

My phone buzzes, pulling me from my thoughts.

*Hazel* – Lunch at Joe's

The text is in our group chat, which means Olivia, Hayes, and Jett will also be there. This also means either Hazel has a hair-brained idea that will get us arrested and thrown in jail, or she and Hayes finally eloped, and they're married.

Jett and Olivia are back on right now, so maybe it has something to do with them. It's weird; seeing Jett with random girls from campus doesn't really bother me, maybe because of his 'one and done' rule. But seeing him and Olivia together is really hard. I avoid the house a little more when they're together, practice a little longer, and study a little later.

Everyone's 'Yes' texts and their meal ideas ignite a buzzing frenzy on my phone. A few neighboring students shoot me dirty looks, and I can't help but think they're definitely here to understand chemical reactions and not just pass with a C for credits.

*Me* – I'll be there.

Then, I silence my phone and throw it deep into the abyss of my backpack, trying to stifle the incessant vibrating.

●  ●  ●

As I approach the entrance to Joe's, I can't ignore the sinking feeling in the pit of my stomach. The last time I was here was when Jett told me about him and Olivia. I've avoided Joe's ever since. I take a deep, calming breath and pull open the heavy wooden door that leads to my favorite smell in all the world. I inhale again and say to myself, *It's been too long, Joe's, man, have I missed you.* The smell of their fresh bread fills my senses, and I savor it. The sweetness of their freshly baked cookies is intoxicating.

I find everyone at our usual table and make my way over to them.

"Did you guys order?"

"Yes," Hazel replies. "Everyone put their order in the group chat, but you didn't, so I just got you a turkey with avocado. Jett said it was your favorite."

"Thanks. So, what's the occasion?" I ask. "Are we getting arrested tonight or attending your and Haye's wedding?" I motion between them, then add as I look at my watch, "Whichever one it is, I need to be at practice in three hours, so it has to be quick."

"Hayes and I just started officially dating a week ago. Can you not marry us off yet?"

I ask Hayes, "How many times have you asked her to marry you this week?"

"Twelve times, twice a day," he answers with zero hesitation in his voice.

I give Hazel one of my famous 'I told you' grins.

"We're not getting married," she says and looks to Olivia.

"I'm pregnant!" Olivia screeches, and then she and Hazel continue to screech.

I immediately look to Jett. "Are they kidding?"

He shakes his head no, but he doesn't say no like he's disappointed, more afraid of my disappointment like a kid who accidentally threw a baseball through the living-room window.

"Are you the father?"

Before he can even get a word out, Olivia interrupts, her tone sharp and defensive, "Of course, he's the father; who else would be the father? What kind of question is that?" Her words hang in the air like an impending storm, thick with tension, ready to break at any moment. The split-second silence that follows feels charged as if everyone is bracing themselves for the inevitable downpour.

"Calm down," I say, surrendering my hands in a gesture of peace, breaking the tense silence. "I just mean you two are so on again, off again. I didn't know if you were on right now or off. I stopped keeping track."

Jett's jaw tightens, his eyes narrowing. "That's a shitty thing to say." His voice is low but sharp, each word clipped and deliberate. The restrained anger makes it clear – he's choosing her, and I feel the crack widening between our friendship.

"It's the truth. Sorry if the truth stings a little. If your friends can't be honest with you, then who can?" I say, holding up my hand for Hayes to high-five, but he just looks to Hazel, and she gives him a disapproving nod, so I high-five myself.

Hazel clears her throat; her eyes move between Jett and me. "Um, am I missing something?" Her voice is light, almost cautious, like she's trying to ease the tension without fully knowing how. It's as if she's caught in the middle of something she doesn't understand. Of course, she doesn't understand – how could she? I've never told any of them about how I've always felt about Jett.

"What about football?" I ask Jett, ignoring her question. I do not do confrontation, but apparently, today, I do.

"What about football?" Jett retorts.

"How are you going to play and raise a baby?"

"Olivia will live where I play."

"You think Olivia is going to move to…" I pause, trying to think of the worst place to live where there is an NFL team. "You think Olivia is going to move to Minnesota away from her family and friends with a newborn only to get buried in fifty feet of snow every winter so you can play football?"

"Yes, I will if that's where he gets drafted. I'll move to fifty feet of snow with *our* baby to be a family." Her voice is resolute. Her eyes reflect determination as she responds to my question that was never intended for her.

"Well, then, I guess y'all have it all worked out. Congratulations. I can't wait." I look at my watch and push my seat back. "I have to go. I have practice."

"Wait, you said practice was in three hours. We haven't

even gotten our lunch." Hazel's voice is on the verge of panic.

"I'm not hungry," I say, my voice strained as I get up and take a step towards the door. But I pause and look back to the table, standing over everyone because, apparently, today is the day I embrace confrontation. "You want to know what's shitty? The fact that everyone at this table already knows you two are having a baby, and I didn't. When did I become the outcast of the bunch? Why are we all at lunch when this big announcement is only for me? Next time, do me a favor and just send me a text."

The same shitty feeling from the last time I left this fucking restaurant washes over me, but this time, it solidifies my worst fears. There will never be a future for Jett and me. He and Olivia are having a baby and starting a family.

My heart feels like it's shattering into a million pieces as I step onto the sidewalk, the cool air hitting my flushed cheeks. The realization stings: I need to figure out how to be happy for them, or I will lose the only real group of friends I've ever had. The thought of being without them feels like a knife twisting in my gut, and I blink back the tears that threaten to spill over, determined to keep it together just a little longer.

# Chapter 14

## JETT

I thought that of all the people in my life, Kadin would've been the one to be supportive and happy for me—for us. But whatever just happened was not a best friend being happy. It was a shit show, and I don't know how to feel about any of it right now. My chest tightens with a mix of confusion and hurt, like the ground has been pulled out from under me.

Kadin's reaction wasn't just unexpected; it was a gut punch. The disappointment cuts deep, leaving me reeling and questioning everything I thought I knew about our friendship.

I glance around the table, taking in the bewildered expression of my friends. "Why is she so mad?" I ask, breaking the awkward silence hanging between us.

Hayes frowns, echoing my confusion. "What just happened?"

Hazel looking completely thrown off, shrugs. "I have no idea," she admits, her tone reminding me of someone asked to solve a math problem in front of the class with no prep.

Olivia doesn't even look up, her voice flat and direct. "She's jealous."

I lean back into my seat, shaking my head. "I don't think

she's jealous," I argue, which, in hindsight, is probably not my brightest moment.

"She's jealous," Olivia repeats, this time with more force, her eyes locking onto mine, daring me to contradict her again.

I shift uncomfortably, my brow furrowed. "She's jealous you're having a baby?" I ask, genuinely baffled.

Olivia finally looks up, meeting my eyes. "First off, *we're* having a baby," she corrects. "And second, she's not jealous I'm having a baby. She's jealous I'm having a baby with you."

I shake my head, running my hand through my hair. "That's ridiculous. Kadin and I are best friends, that's it."

"Is it ridiculous?" Hazel chimes in, her voice soft but challenging.

I look between the two of them, feeling like I'm suddenly on trial for a crime I didn't commit. "Isn't it?" I counter, feeling the tension growing.

Hazel and Olivia share a glance before Olivia sighs, her tone softer now. "You probably should've told her you were just friends back in kindergarten."

I shift in my seat, guilt starting to gnaw at the edges of my confusion "Should I call her?" I ask, genuinely concerned now.

Hazel shakes her head slightly, resting it against Hayes's shoulder as she sighs. "No, she'll be fine; she'll work through it."

I look at the two of them sitting there all in love and can't help but feel like I've been sucked into an alternate universe where Hayes and Hazel are dating, Kadin hates me, and my on-and-off girlfriend is pregnant and says she'll move wherever I get drafted. How did all this happen?

Testing fate, I ask, "Can I just say an observation out loud without everyone getting pissed at me or saying I'm defending Kadin?"

"I'm game," Hayes says because he is a shit disturber.

"Well," I say, playing with my napkin, trying not to waiver in my belief that Kadin wouldn't be that mad over just Olivia being pregnant. I point to Hayes and Hazel. "You two are together now, and we all know nothing will come between you, or one of you will end up in jail."

They smile at each other, and it's really hard not to laugh.

"Olivia and I are together having a baby. Has anyone thought maybe Kadin feels like there's no longer a place for her in our group? We've always been the five musketeers, but now we're two couples and a fifth wheel."

"You're not wrong," Hazel agrees. "I never thought how this would make her feel." Her voice is empathetic and full of understanding.

I glance at Olivia, hoping for some kind of clarity or validation, but she's distant, her attention fixed on the work outside, watching people walk by as if they hold the answers she's searching for.

"Are you okay?" I ask her, rubbing her leg, trying to assure her I'm here and I love her. Kadin will be fine, and I'll be fine, and she'll be fine.

"Yeah, I'm okay. And, you're right, it's a lot for Kadin to process."

Hayes chimes in, "Can we eat already? I'm starving."

"Yes, hurry and eat. We have an appointment at a baby store in forty-five minutes," Hazel says.

"What kind of appointment and what baby store? What are we buying?" I look to Olivia for help, but she just shrugs.

"You know I'm a broke college student, right?" I continue, "Remember the 'I'll be happy living in a cardboard box just so long as we're together' speech you gave me the other day?"

She just shakes her head in acceptance with a huge grin that lights up the room and says, "You know Hazel. There's no stopping her plans."

# Chapter 15

## OLIVIA

Hazel is holding a small wastebasket for me as I retch uncontrollably. It's been two weeks since I saw the doctor, and I seem to be feeling worse as the days pass. Each step toward the doctor's office feels like an eternity; my body is racked with nausea and exhaustion. I have missed school for the past two weeks, putting me in danger of being dropped. The constant pounding in my head makes it impossible to concentrate in class. My migraines are relentless; before I was pregnant, I could take pills for relief, but now I'm forced to fight through the pain, which only worsens my vomiting.

I haven't even told my parents yet. I want to tell them in person, but with the way I've been feeling, I'm starting to wonder how long I can keep this a secret.

Last week, Jett was able to drive me to my check-up. He is concerned by my non-stop migraines and vomiting and how it could be affecting our baby. Last visit, the doctor ordered a slew of tests, hoping for some answers. Today is results day. Jett wanted to be here with me, but he had a big test and a mandatory football meeting that he couldn't miss, leaving me in the not-so-calm hands of my cousin.

"I feel like I'm here more than I'm home," I say through fits of heaving.

Hazel silently rubs my back in slow and steady circles, her usual jokes and playful energy absent. She gently hands me a water bottle, her expression tight with worry, eyes scanning my face for any sign of relief.

"I know, Olivia, but we'll have all the answers we need today, and we'll get you feeling better in no time."

I nod, trying to muster as much optimism as she has, but deep down, I can't shake the overwhelming feeling of despair that suffocates me when I'm alone. Does Hazel truly believe her own words? At this moment, I can't fathom ever feeling better again.

Dr. Stacey walks in, holding her iPad. Without niceties or hesitation, she begins, "Olivia, you're here in Texas for school. Is that correct?" she asks, looking up briefly from her screen.

I nod and reply, "Yes, ma'am."

She taps something on the iPad, her finger moving in a rhythm that feels far too calm for the tension in the room. "And, your parents are where?"

"California," I answer, my fingers gripping the edge of the exam table.

Her eyes meet mine for a moment. "And your cousin and boyfriend are your support system?"

"Yes, ma'am, and a few other friends we live with," I say, trying to keep my voice steady.

She raises an eyebrow. "Like at a party house?"

I shake my head, a nervous laugh escaping before I realize how out of place it sounds. "No, ma'am. There are just four of us. We grew up together. We don't host parties. I'm sorry; what does any of this have to do with my results?"

Dr. Stacey stops tapping, her gaze softening in a way that makes my heart drop. She sighs quietly before saying, "Olivia, we got your MRIs and bloodwork back. Your MRI is showing you have Glioblastoma—"

Hazel interrupts, "I'm sorry, what? We are not medical students. Can you tell us in plain English?"

My doctor continues, "Glioblastoma is an aggressive form of brain cancer…"

I hear my doctor's voice, but the words are a blur, like background noise in a movie, or when you're doing chores and you just have music playing for noise. It's sort of like my soul has detached from my body, hovering above us in disbelief. I try to rub away the numbness, to grasp the reality of what's being said, but no matter how hard I try to focus, it's like listening to a Charlie Brown cartoon – sounds without meaning, surreal and distant.

Not knowing if I interrupt her or if she's done talking, I say, "Wait, I'm sorry. I think I need a minute to process what you just said."

Silence fills the room for what feels like an eternity, but Hazel gets up from the chair she was sitting in and moves over to the bed thing I'm sitting on. She hoists herself up, and I can hear the wrinkles on the protective paper gown as she scoots close to me.

"Doctor, can you start from the beginning, please?"

"Olivia's type of cancer is very rare but also very aggressive. The average life expectancy is fifteen months. We can add to her life expectancy with chemotherapy and radiation therapy, but even with all treatments exhausted, we will only add four to six months to your life expectancy.

"Wait, wait, wait!" Hazel yells. "Are you saying Olivia is dying no matter what?"

"What I'm saying is even with treatment, only five percent of patients survive."

Hazel claps her hands together as she jumps off the bed with unwavering optimism. "Okay, so what I'm hearing is we have a five percent chance of beating this. When do we start treatment?" Her words are infused with enthusiasm, embodying the essence of her character—always glass-half-full, ready to take on the world. Hazel is the picture of unwavering hope. But today, as much as I love and appreciate her optimism, I know I have to burst her bubble as my stark reality must take precedence over her dreams.

Holding up my hand, I ask, "How will treatment affect my baby?

"Chemotherapy increases the risk of birth defects in unborn babies and can lead to miscarriage."

"I'm fourteen weeks pregnant; if I die before my due date, can you deliver the baby early?"

"Yes, knowing your condition, we will deliver the baby c-section regardless, but we can talk more about delivering the baby early if we have to, but as of today, I'm comfortable saying you'll keep the baby until medically necessary."

Hazel's eyes bounce between the two of us as she asks, "Wait, what are you asking, Olivia? What's your thoughts?"

Dr. Stacey raises an eyebrow at me, waiting for my reply.

"Well, I can tell you, without a doubt, I'm not starting chemo until the baby is at term. I'm okay delivering it early and starting chemo soon after that, but I want to make sure it's healthy and strong enough."

"Wait a minute, Olivia." Hazel holds her hands in front of her, fingers spread. "That's..." She pauses, looking at her fingers, and the humor is not lost on me that, first, Hazel is terrible at math and can't add or subtract without using her fingers.

"You're only fourteen weeks pregnant; you still have…" She pauses again and looks at Dr Stacey. "How many more weeks does she have?"

"Twenty-six weeks left."

"That's…" She pauses again to calculate weeks into months, which is impossible for her.

I interject, "That's six and half months left, Hazel, and it's not up for debate. I'm not starting chemo and potentially harming or losing the baby. "I'm going to die regardless; this baby will be my legacy. He or she will be all I have to leave behind for Jett, my parents, and you guys to remember me by." I look down at my legs dangling off the bed and continue, "Hazel, it'll be all you have left to remember me. I really don't want to argue about it. I don't have the energy."

Hazel nods in understanding.

So, I continue, "Doctor, what's next?"

"I'm going to give you a few prescriptions. It'll help with nausea and hopefully allow you some relief from your migraines."

The drive home feels never ending as we sit in silence, watching the landscape pass us by; each new intersection is a reminder of unspoken words. Hazel, usually the optimistic one, is silent, her vibrant personality lost in shattered dreams. It's not fair for me to expect her to fill the void with conversation, knowing her heart is as broken as mine.

"You good?" I ask, breaking our deafening silence.

"No, I'm not good. I'm really shitty." A rouge tear runs down her cheek.

The confession breaks my heart.

"My best friend *(my cousin)* is dying and refusing to do anything about it. I can't talk to my parents about it." She lowers her voice, and I hear a glimmer of acceptance in her voice. "But I understand why you're not telling them; I understand why you're not doing chemo, and I understand your pain outweighs mine; I understand the burden you carry is incomprehensible, and I understand this is about you and not me, and I should be strong for you, and I'm doing a shitty job being strong because this is all pretty fucking shitty."

# Chapter 16

## OLIVIA

Walking into the place I've called home for almost four years feels different today. The atmosphere that greets me, usually familiar and comforting, suddenly feels altered, almost surreal, as my mind struggles to process the news and its implications. There's a profound sense of disconnection where this place, typically a sanctuary or a place for fun and friends, offers me little comfort in my state of shock or sadness.

Jett is sleeping on the couch, sitting up, clearly exhausted, his head hanging forward, resting on his chest in the most awkward position—he clearly didn't intend to fall asleep there. He's been staying up late with me every night, studying to be on track to graduate and working out with the team even though the season is done.

I sit on the edge of the couch cushion, the movement jolting him awake. He blinks, groggy, but instantly alert when he sees me, his concern evident despite the tired lines on his face.

"What did the doctor say?" he asks, his voice thick with sleep but filled with worry.

"I'm going to check on Hayes and give you guys a minute," Hazel says as she walks down the hallway.

I hear her close Hayes's door behind her.

"We need to talk," I say in a shaky voice. I can't cry right now; I need to keep it together.

Jett sits up and pushes his hair off his face. "Olivia, the last time you said that, you told me you were pregnant. Are we having twins?"

"No," I answer, and believe it or not, that question makes me chuckle.

His eyes grow wide. "Triplets?"

I turn to face him and put my hands on both his legs. "I have incurable brain cancer. I'm dying."

Have you ever watched someone's soul leave their body? Me neither, until today. Jett's face goes stark white, like a pristine fabric. His eyes widen, and it seems like he forgets how to breathe for a moment. His mouth opens, but no sound comes out, like he's trying to find the right words in a world that suddenly doesn't make sense anymore.

"I'm sorry, but I don't understand?" he finally stammers, shaking his head in disbelief. "You can't be…dying. We're having a baby, Olivia. We're supposed to have a future."

The room suddenly feels colder, and the air seems heavier, like a dense fog has settled in. Jett's usually warm hands tremble under my surprisingly steady hands.

He blinks rapidly as if trying to wake up from a nightmare. "There has to be something," he insists, his voice shaking. "A Clinical trial, experimental treatments, something. This…this can't be it. There has to be something—"

His voice cracks on the last word, and I watch as tears fill his eyes. He grips my hands tighter, searching for a lifeline.

"I'm pregnant, Jett. That's why there's nothing that can

be done."

The weight of my words linger between us. Jett's jaw tightens, his fingers squeezing around mine.

"So, if you weren't...they could save you?" His voice is barely above a whisper, the question hanging in the air.

"No," I say softly. "They can't, but they could prolong my suffering, and I don't want that. Not for me. Not for you." I pause, taking a breath, and the silence between us is thick with unspoken fears. Then, in an attempt to lighten the mood, I let out a small laugh. "Do you know that I played softball just to make my parents happy growing up?"

Jett blinks, caught off guard by the sudden shift. His eyes widen, then he chuckles, the sound breaking the tension like a sudden burst of sunlight through storm clouds. "Well, you weren't very good, so I'm not surprised."

"Hey." I poke him in the side, laughing as his grin spreads.

I rest my head on his shoulder, and we both exhale, the heaviness lifting just a little. "I graduated high school early to be with Kadin and Hazel...to make them happy. Don't get me wrong, I'm glad I'm here, but sometimes I feel like I've been living my entire life for everyone around me." I look up at him, my voice softening. "You are the only selfish thing I've ever done in my life. And I don't regret it."

"What do you mean?" Jett asks shifting slightly.

"I knew Kadin loved you," I say, playing with the hem of my shirt. "I shouldn't have taken you from her."

Jett strokes my hair. "You didn't. I wanted to be with you."

I lift my head so I can meet his eyes. "I know, but I should've pushed you toward her. I should've given you the choice, but I didn't. I was scared you'd choose her over me." I drop my head on his shoulder again, my voice quieter now. "I just wanted something for myself for once..."

Jett cups my face in his hands, lifting my chin so I have to look at him. "I'd choose you a million times, Olivia."

A small, sad smile forms on my lips. "And I'd choose our baby a million times more."

The silence that follows is deafening. Jett's shoulders slump as he rests his head on mine. The chill of our tears mingle as his fall to my face and mine onto his shoulder. We hold onto each other, trying to find strength in our shared sorrow.

# Chapter 17

## KADIN

I thought walking into the house I'd been avoiding the past several days would feel uncomfortable, like I was an outsider and didn't belong here anymore, but a gentle wave of warmth greets me, accompanied by the fresh smell of coffee.

"I'll take a cup, too," I yell to Hazel, who is standing in the kitchen wrapped up in a hug from Hayes.

"You're home," Olivia says from the couch.

"Of course I'm home. Last time I checked, I still live here," I say, trying to act like the last time I saw everyone, I didn't storm out like a jealous girlfriend or overbearing parent. I've been back and forth on the two scenarios and I'm hoping I gave off parent vibes, not girlfriend vibes, but I'm certainly not asking my friends.

"Don't act like you've not been MIA for the past week," Hazel yells from the kitchen, clutching her coffee with two hands as if someone is going to take it from her.

"What's going on?" I ask as I sit down on the couch next to Olivia. But as my gaze meets hers, there's a noticeable shift in her appearance and demeanor. Gone is the usual glow she exudes, replaced by worry and sadness.

"Are you mad at me?" I ask, ripping off the Band-Aid.

"Am I mad at you? Why would I be mad at you? For looking out for your best friend and making sure he's not giving up on the only dream he's ever had for an on-again off, off-again girlfriend and a baby?"

"Olivia, I didn't mean it like that."

"Why? You're right. We have been on again and off again for a year now; why would anyone take us seriously?

"I didn't mean it like that either."

"Kadin, I'm not mad at you for being truthful and looking out for Jett. He's always been your closest friend. I'm not going to take that from you. I want you to know that no matter what happens between Jett and me or Hayes and Hazel, you will always have a place in our friend group."

"Don't worry about me. I'm so busy with soccer, and the girls have been begging me to stay at the soccer house until we graduate in a few months. I'm all good," I say, forcing a smile and trying to sound like my typical happy-go-lucky self. My voice wavers slightly, but I hope they don't notice.

Inside, I feel the awkwardness gnawing at me. Being in the house with two couples just makes every moment feel like I'm an outsider in my own home.

Hazel comes and sits down on the smaller sofa to the left of us and hands me my coffee. Her eyes meet Olivia's, and a silent understanding passes between them, a wordless interaction that speaks louder than words.

In that fleeting moment, the weight of their connection that I'll never share hangs heavy in the air. With a subtle nod from Olivia, Hazel takes a breath and starts to speak.

"Olivia has an incurable, cancerous brain tumor…"

There isn't much else I can hear through the ringing in my

ears. I think Hazel is continuing to talk, but I can't comprehend anything she's saying, and in this pivotal moment, I know that our lives will be forever defined by before we knew Olivia had cancer and after.

• • •

I look at my phone and whisper to myself, *"It's only 1 a.m."* The past several hours hang heavy in the air and has robbed me of any potential for sleep.

There's a faint knock on my door, so quiet I think I may be imagining it.

"Come in," I whisper, my voice catching in my throat.

My door slowly opens, then stops halfway. "I'm awake," I say a little louder this time, sitting up in bed and rubbing the dried-up tears from my eyes. The silhouette of Hazel emerges from the hallway, barely visible against the soft light behind her.

"What's wrong? Why are you awake? Why are you here and not with Hayes?" My voice is sleepy even though sleep is the furthest thing from my mind.

"I can't sleep," she whispers. "And Hayes snores."

I manage a weak smile but lie back down, staring at the ceiling. "Yeah, me either."

She walks to the opposite side of my bed and pulls my covers back. She slips in and immediately turns onto her side to face me. She puts her arm under the pillow to prop herself up and then pulls the covers back over us.

I turn to my side to meet her eyes. The space between us feels like the only safe place left in the world. I let out a long breath, but I can't hold back anymore. "She going to die, isn't she?" I ask in a whisper, my throat tightening with each word.

Hazel's face twists in pain, but she doesn't look away. "I don't know, but I think so."

I immediately start to cry. "Why didn't you tell me she was so sick?"

Hazel reaches out, tucking a strand of my dark hair behind my ear and gently wipes a tear from my cheek. "I didn't know it was this bad, Kadin," she says, her voice barely above a whisper. "We thought it was the pregnancy, and you've been so busy with soccer you didn't need the distraction."

"This is a little bit more than a distraction, Hazel," I say, my voice cracking "You've made me feel like even more of an outsider than I already do."

Hazel's eyes fill with tears too, and she pulls me closer, her hand resting softly on my arm. "I'm so sorry," she whispers. "But I'm glad you're home."

# Chapter 18

## HAZEL

I slowly pry open my heavy eyelids, and the harsh reality of the day ahead comes crashing down on me, along with the lingering sorrow from last night. I feel around Kadin's bed for her, only to realize she's already gone, which makes me feel better that she's keeping some of her habits. This cannot affect her soccer.

With a weary sigh, I muster the energy to swing my legs over the bed and slowly walk to the kitchen, surprised to see Olivia sitting at the island while Hayes and Kadin cook breakfast.

"I was just going to wake you," Hayes says as he makes his way to me before kissing me gently on my lips and handing me my coffee.

I stand there, taking in the scene. Everyone turns to look at me. Watching them, you'd never know my cousin is dying from cancer.

I run my hand over my face and walk to an empty seat at the island. "Kadin, why aren't you at soccer?"

"I have a game later, you know that."

"Morning workout?"

"I'm skipping it."

"How do you feel?" I ask Olivia as I get up to grab her pills.

She grabs my arm to stop me and says, "I actually feel okay today, no morning sickness. Jett already gave me my pills. He's in the shower. Sit down and wait for breakfast."

Hayes slides a plate full of eggs, potatoes, and toast across the island toward me. I look up at him and slide it over to Olivia so she can eat before me. She slides it back in my direction and looks away. I shake my head and shove a fork full of eggs in my mouth.

"We go home to California in two weeks for winter break. Do we have a plan?" I ask.

Olivia clears her throat then answers, "I'm dropping out of school and will stay in California with my parents. Jett is coming home with me."

"What about football?" Hayes asks, his face etched with concern.

"Football is over for the season; we won the championship, remember? And it's my senior year. There's no more football for me," Jett says as he enters the common area from Olivia's room.

Hayes leans forward, his eyes narrowed as he stares at Jett. "So, that's it? You're just…walking away from going pro?" His voice is edged with disbelief, the weight of his question hanging in the air. "You're really throwing away your shot at the NFL?"

"Yeah, Hayes. That's it. I'm having a baby; what else do you want from me? I'm staying home to help my fiancé fight brain cancer and carry our baby. Then I will take care of our baby so my wife can enjoy what little time she has left with me and our baby."

Kadin raises her hand, and we all look at her, apparently

giving her permission to speak because she blurts out, "I missed a lot of details last night; did I miss the marriage part?"

I'm shaking my head no. "I missed that too. Do you two care to explain?"

Olivia speaks up, "Jett proposed last night. It's always been my dream to walk down the aisle with my dad, and I'd like our baby to know that her parents loved each other enough to be married before she was born."

"She?" I ask.

"Call it a mother's intuition."

"It's going to be a boy," Hayes argues.

Ignoring Hayes, I study Jett, trying to get a read on how he's really feeling about everything. A few short weeks ago, he helped take his college team to the championships, and now he's being thrust into an alternate reality that no one ever imagined for him. I know he loves Olivia, but this thing between them never seemed like it would end in marriage.

"Okay, so we plan a wedding, a baby shower, and graduation parties," I say.

"And a funeral," Olivia cuts in.

All our heads snap in her direction, and she continues, "Listen, guys, I'm dying. Please stop tiptoeing around it. If you think I'm allowing our mothers to handle the details"—she motions around the room to all of us—"you're sadly mistaken, so planning a funeral will be on that list."

I completely ignore what she just said. "When we leave for winter break, I'm staying home with Olivia. I'll finish school online; my degree means nothing at this point."

Hayes turns his head so fast I think he's going to get whiplash. "You can't drop out of school, Hazel."

"Yes, I can. I already withdrew from my classes next semester, so it's done, and there's nothing to talk about."

Kadin interrupts, "So, again, the two of you drop out of school without telling me. Do you think I'm staying in Texas alone? What the hell, Hazel."

"You can stay here with Hayes," I retort.

The two of them look at each other.

"No thanks; I'm not getting left with the consolation prize." Kadin folds her arms.

Hayes raises his hands in mock defense, a playful grin tugging at his lips. "Hey, no need to throw out insults, Kadin," he says, his voice lighter now.

"Stop, you two. Seriously. Kadin, what do you want to do? You need to stay here for soccer; the season isn't over. Jett's season is over. He's coming home. I'm doing nothing here, so I'm going home."

Kadin interrupts, "What about Tate?"

"We broke up like two weeks ago."

"Seriously, I'm completely out of the loop. Y'all might as well move home and leave me here. I'm basically on an island alone."

I give her a dirty look and say, "You done with your pity party because you could be the one with a huge tumor in your head."

"Oh, way to hit her where it hurts," Hayes cheers me on.

"Um, I'm right here," Olivia says as she raises her hand.

"Too soon?" I ask with a smile I usually reserve for my mom when I'm in trouble.

"So that settles it," Hayes says, breaking the tension. "Kadin and I will finish out the school year and go home after graduation."

"Speak for yourself, Hayes; I'm going home to be with Olivia."

"For fuck sake, you girls are impossible," he says as he rubs his hands over his face. "Looks like we are all dropping out of school. Are we telling our parents now or once we're home?"

"*Home*," we all shout in unison.

"At least you girls can agree on one thing," Jett says.

# Chapter 19

## HAZEL

As if on cue, everyone's alarms start ringing simultaneously on our phones. Kadin's alarm blares relentlessly through our thin shared wall, while Olivia's alarm either prompts her to get out of bed immediately or is silenced by Jett to allow her just a little more sleep. Predicting Olivia's morning demeanor is always a gamble; she might wake up feeling fantastic and ready to seize the day, or she could be so unwell she spends the entire day confined to her bedroom. So, we're literally taking this illness and pregnancy day by day.

Kadin's alarm is still going off, and I've been up and moving for at least ten minutes. I walk to our shared wall and bang on it. "Get up, the Uber will be here in forty-five minutes."

I hear her moan into her pillow, the telltale sign of a hangover.

Kadin, Hayes, and I went out last night, one last hurrah, with some of the friends we've made over the last four years here at Lincoln College. Yesterday was our last day here as students. The news came as a surprise to all our friends and teachers. The five of us showed up here wet behind the ears and scared as hell to be away from home, and four years later, the five and a half of us are leaving adults. Hayes will finish the required classes to receive his business degree and go to work with his father immediately. That was always part of the plan, except the degree wasn't supposed to be from an online school. Kadin will enroll at our local community college and try to get scouted that way, but that's a wish and a hope. The odds of being scouted for the Olympics at a community college are as slim as my mom being supportive of me dropping out of college halfway through my senior year.

Jett will (hopefully) move in with Olivia. Of course, her parents will decide once we tell them what's been happening over the past several weeks in Texas.

And, as far as me, I'll cherish every moment with Olivia, wearing out my welcome at my aunt and uncle's house. I'll be by her side when she gives birth to her baby, which promises to be the most memorable day of my life. I'll stand beside her as she marries Jett, and I'll hold her hand as she reaches her final moments. I'll witness the raw emotions of my aunt's heartbreak, and I'll stand before our families when we lay her to rest and always promise to remember what an amazing friend, cousin, sister, daughter, and mother she was, no matter how short her life.

Looking down at my phone, I yell, "Five minutes. Everyone better be up and ready to go."

"Shut up," Kadin groans.

"I will leave you behind, Kadin," I yell back.

Hayes knocks on my door and enters without permission. "Um, come in," I answer.

"I'm already in," he says, stating the obvious, looking at me like I'm his prey.

"What if I wasn't dressed?"

"I've seen you naked like three times, and you've slept with me every night the past few weeks."

"Four times. We've had sex four times. I know each time was 'accidental'," I said, using air quotes. "But it's still something. It was still sex, and you never saw my whole body, just parts. And when I've slept with you lately, it's not been naked."

His eyes widen playfully and he says, "Okay, Hazel, you keep telling yourself that."

"Keep telling myself what?" Playfulness dances in my voice.

"That our sex didn't mean anything and that I haven't seen you fully naked."

"Why is everything a joke with you, Hayes?"

"Who said I'm joking?" His voice is low and serious as he steps closer, closing the distance between us.

My back hits the dresser, now empty and waiting for the next round of college students. The proximity sends my heart racing and my body temperature soaring.

I struggle to steady my breathing, managing only a whisper, "What are you doing? We don't have time for this."

His eyes lock onto mine, intense and unwavering. "Making sure you know you're not a joke to me," he murmurs, his voice a mix of resolve and raw emotion. The tension between us crackles, filling the space with an electric charge that leaves me breathless.

"You're impossible, Hayes Emmerson," I say in a strangled voice. "What do you want?"

"I want you, Hazel," he says, his voice steady yet filled with an undercurrent of intensity. "But I came in here to see if you needed help since you have no intention of ever coming back. I figured you had a lot of stuff packed."

How does someone drop a bombshell like '*Oh hi, I want you, Hazel*' and then carry on like normal?

Completely caught off guard and flustered, all I can manage

is, "Oh, okay. Thanks, but I'm only taking my one suitcase. I'm assuming our dads will come back and pack everything up."

Nervousness knots my stomach, making me question all my decisions—not my choice to stay in California with Olivia, but my decision not to tell my parents, at least to give them a heads-up. I'm an adult. I can make my own decisions, but I never keep secrets from my mom; it's not in my nature. But this wasn't my secret to tell.

And then there's Hayes, a choice that's left my life spinning out of control. How did we get from me chasing him in elementary school, to him beating up boys in high school who talked to me, to me watching him flirt his way through the first three years of college, to him cock blocking me, and now we're exclusive? My heart pounds as I try to make sense of everything.

"Hazel… Hazel… Hazel!" Hayes shouts.

I look up at him.

"Are you listening to me?"

"No." I shake my head. "I'm not, I'm sorry. I'm just concerned about showing up at home without warning my parents of what's happening here. My mom is going to be disappointed."

Hayes takes me in his arms and rests his head on top of mine. The mood has shifted, though. He's no longer possessive and intensive; he's warm and loving, and he smells so good.

His voice is quieter now. "Hazel. Sure, your mom will be disappointed when you tell her you're dropping out of school, but that will be nothing compared to the fear and sorrow for Olivia. It'll all work out."

I pull myself away from him and look up to him, "Hayes, my cousin is dying. Nothing is going to work out."

"You have to be strong for Olivia. You can fall apart in

private or with me, but at the point you give up, Olivia will give up, and she has to believe that she will beat this to stay strong for the baby."

"I know." I rest my forehead on his chest. "This is going to kill me, Hayes."

He lifts my chin to make eye contact with me. "No one is ever promised a perfect life, and we're definitely not promised a full life, so don't let this tragedy define you. You have amazing parents; you still have Kadin and your younger cousins. I'm not saying any of them will replace Olivia because I know no one will ever replace her for you, but in time, your relationship with them will ease some of the loss."

I just shake my head in agreement. He kisses my forehead, lifts his head to the sky, and yells, "Let's go, people. We have a plane to catch, and the Uber will be here any minute."

• • •

We land at 8 p.m. local time, and once I power up my phone, I have at least twenty text messages.

*Maddy* – Hey, I saw on social media you're back in town. Meet us at 6-Dogs Pub.

*Kallie* – OMG, you're back in California! Meet us at the Pub.

*Elliot* – Hey, stranger. I hear you are in town for winter break. We'll be at the pub tonight. I hope you stop by. I know some of the girls are going crazy to see you.

I look at Kadin. "Did everyone text you?"

"No!"

"How does everyone know we're in town?"

"I don't know." She shrugs.

"Who put something on social media that we're in town?" I ask, looking across the row of airplane seats.

Hayes raises his hand. "Guilty."

"Seriously, Hayes, take down the post. Our parents think we're coming home in two days. If they find out…"

Kadin interrupts me, "What? What are they going to do? Ground us? We're adults; stop stressing about our parents."

I know she's right, and I know I'm an adult, but the fear of disappointing my parents didn't vanish the day I turned eighteen. But I ignore the rational, mature side of my brain and ask Kadin, "Are you thinking what I'm thinking?"

"No, I'm not. You know I woke up with a hangover because you had to say bye to everyone, and now you want me to wake up with another one when we have to show our faces at home and break everyone's heart?"

"Yes! Yes, that's exactly what I want!" My voice trembles, and I'm not sure if it's from excitement or sorrow. "I want to make as many good memories as possible with Olivia," I say, my voice breaking, and I know it's from sorrow now. I hate talking about Olivia dying, it's almost as if saying it makes it more of a reality – a reality I refuse to accept. "To have one last night of fun in our hometown before everything changes."

I pause, swallowing hard. My throat burning from the emotions that have been building for days. Maybe even weeks. "What's wrong with wanting to create memories? She didn't go with us last night. Maybe she'll say hi to everyone tonight before her world shifts; before she's known only for her cancer."

Kadin shakes her head with a grin. "Okay, let's do it!"

When it's our aisles' turn to deplane, we walk towards the exit in a straight line. I turn around to walk backward so I can face everyone "I've had at least twenty people text me to say how excited they are to see us," I say, glancing at everyone's reactions.

"Me too!" Hayes pipes in, cutting me off with a grin that matches Kadin's.

I spin back around to face forward since we're almost off the plane. The energy still buzzes between us, and I can't hold back. "Soooooo, Olivia, are you up to stopping by the pub to see everyone? We can have some fun and make memories on our first night back in town."

"I can't drink," Olivia reminds me, her voice a mix of humor and reality.

"Duh, you're pregnant, not dying," I shoot back, winking as I point at her.

Olivia just chuckles and shrugs, but I don't miss the brief flicker of hesitation before she turns to Jett, and asks, "What do you think?"

He meets her eyes and tries his best to hide his excitement, but it's not working. "I'm down if you are."

"Let's do it!" Olivia says with a deep inhale. "Promise me," she says, as she points to each of us. "Promise you won't tell anyone that I'm sick tonight. Let's just celebrate that Jett and I are having a baby. No sympathy, no sad looks – just fun. Okay?"

"No sad looks," I promise her.

Kadin punches the air with her fist and whisper shouts, "Yes!"

•  •  •

As we step into the pub, I'm instantly transported back to the days when we dreamed of hanging out here with our friends, but instead, we all left for Texas. I'm so pleased we made the last-minute decision to book a hotel so we could drop off our suitcases and change before heading to the bar. We'll head to our houses first thing tomorrow. But tonight, it's all about having fun.

The pub exudes a cozy and inviting atmosphere. The lights are dim, but you can still see the wood furnishings, the row of pool tables, and dartboards in the back.

Hayes enters first, and the cheers erupt with enthusiasm and excitement. It feels like we never left. We still know almost everyone in town, and it's like nothing's changed since high school. Everyone else either stayed home, went to the local community college, or started working straight after graduation. It's pretty much just the five of us who left, as if we're the only ones who ventured out.

The only real difference now is that we can all legally drink, no more relying on those terrible fake IDs I used to get us. The sense of familiarity washes over me, but it's a little surreal, too. We've all grown up in some ways, yet in this moment, it's like we've stepped back in time.

Kadin follows Hayes in, and the cheers are replaced by the screeching of her old high-school soccer teammates. They rush toward her, forming a circle like they would do at the end of the game when they would demolish the competition.

And I know that's the last I'll see of Kadin tonight – maybe even the last time I see her for a while. She has her soccer friends here, her family. With the tension between her and Jett, I'm not sure what's going to happen next, but that's a problem for another day.

I stay close to Olivia as Jett enters because he is a star on our football team and part of the college team that won the championship, and I don't want Olivia to get banged up. I push Jett and say, "Go ahead; I'll stay back here with her."

He looks back to Olivia and says, "You, okay?"

"Go ahead," she says as she motions with her head.

Just as I suspected, everyone rushes over to him, embracing him in hugs, fist bumps, and pats on the back. It's mayhem, and it takes me back to the night we won the championship game, and Tate fucked everything up between us. Snapping myself out of memory lane, I take a deep breath, look at Olivia, and say, "Ready?"

She nods.

"Remember, you're pregnant, not dying." I wink at her, and she shoves me.

I try to sneak past the excitement around Hayes, Kadin and Jett, but no such luck. It's hard for me just to blend in. Olivia and I are instantly engulfed in hugs and kisses and drinks spilled on our hair, and it's a fucking mess, but I honestly don't care for myself. I've missed my friends, I've missed my home, and I've missed my parents. I'm so happy to be home right now. I raise my head from above the crowd and see Elliot standing at the bar, holding a beer in one hand and a margarita in the other. He raises it to me, and I wiggle myself free from the girls, run over to him, and throw my arms around him, spilling the margarita on both of us as he tries to hold them up safe from my embrace. Laughing, he sets the drink on the bar and pulls me into a proper hug, his familiar warmth wrapping around me.

Elliot has always been my special friend – the one I didn't have to share with the of the rest of the group. He asked me to dance in high school when Hayes, who was supposed to be my date, wandered off with someone else, and ever since then, he's been my safe place, the person I could vent to without worry that it would get back to everyone else.

"Hazel Jones, did you miss me?" Elliot asks, flashing his familiar, easy smile.

"I missed you more than anyone," I reply, meaning every word.

He kisses my head the way he always has. As I pull back slightly, I catch a glimpse of Hayes watching us.

"What's that about?" Elliot asks, gesturing in Hayes's direction.

"It's new," I say, shrugging a little as I sip my drink. "We're just seeing where this goes, you know. It seems like our timing has been off since we were kids. Maybe it's different now."

Elliot raises an eyebrow, then glances over at Hayes again. "Well, by the way, he's watching us; he's not just seeing where this goes," he says with a chuckle. He lifts his drink toward Hayes in a mock toast from across the bar, and I can't help but laugh as well.

• • •

Several hours have slipped away, and I'm drunk. I scan the pub, trying to find my Olivia, and I'm relieved when I spot her seated in a booth with six other girls. She's drinking water, and I can tell they're gushing over baby talk. Jett, Hayes, Elliot, and some guy I don't recognize are playing pool. I leave my friends, who I've been dancing with all night, and walk off the dance floor over to Hayes and shout at him, "I'm drunk, and it's like two am our time. Can we go soon?"

"This was your idea, princess, and now you want to leave?"

Fueled by liquid courage and a little stupidly, I shake my head at him, saying, "Oh, I get it. Since we're home now, you're going to be an asshole to me? Fuck you, Hayes, I don't need you. I was trying to be polite. The girls and I are leaving."

Elliot drops his stick and rushes to my side, "I'll take you home."

"We're not going home tonight; we're staying at a hotel. Can you drive us?"

"Of course, anything for you." He puts his hand on my lower back and turns me around to lead me out of the pub.

Just then, I feel Elliot get tugged away from me and I look back to see Hayes has one arm in a fist pulled back, ready to hit Elliot. I jump between them and scream, "What the fuck, Hayes? What are you doing?"

Hayes shoves me away from the middle of them and proceeds to hit Elliot in the jaw. I grab Hayes's face and scream, "What is your problem? Stop hitting him!"

I run to Elliot, who's lying on the floor, and touch his face. Hayes grabs me by my sweater and pulls me from the floor.

"Get off the floor, Hazel."

"Why did you do that?" I ask him, tears flowing down my face. At this point, I can't decipher if I'm crying because I'm mad at Hayes, mad at myself, or because I'm tired and drunk and just want to sleep.

"You know why; now get outside and wait for me."

"The fuck I will," I scream in his face, my voice raw with anger and pain as I jab my finger into his chest. "You're not my keeper, Hayes! Stop doing this to me. I've watched you flaunt other girls in front of me for years, and one night, I talk to a friend from high school, and you beat him to a bloody pulp. This right here"—I motion between us—"this is not love; this is possession. And I'm not your possession."

My heart races, each beat echoing the tumult of emotions swirling inside me. Tears blur my vision, but I refuse to let them fall. I'm shaking, not just from rage but from the deep hurt of his actions. The sting of betrayal cuts deep, each word a desperate plea for him to understand the havoc he's wreaking on my heart.

His eyes widen in shock, but I don't care. My chest heaves as I struggle to catch my breath, the weight of my words hanging heavily in the air between us. The raw, unfiltered emotion I've held back for so long finally bursts free, leaving no room for misunderstanding.

Jett comes up to me and pulls me off Hayes, "Hazel, you're drunk; let's go."

I shove Jett off me with all the strength I can muster. "No, fuck you too!" I scream, my voice shaking with a mix of fury and exhaustion. "You've stood by for years, watching while Hayes played his games, and I'm tired of it. I'm tired of both of you."

My chest heaves as I catch my breath, the adrenaline surging through my veins. The look of surprise and hurt in Jett's eyes only fuels my anger. For years, he's been the silent witness, never stepping in, never challenging Hayes, allowing the torment to continue. I feel that the betrayal isn't just from Hayes but from Jett, too, for his complacency and silent complicity. Then I scream at nothing, and I realize I've completely lost my mind, standing in a pub in my hometown with all my childhood friends to witness. I try to make my way through the now-silent crowd of people to the front door, only to be stopped by the cops.

"Fuck, cops," I mumble to myself.

# Chapter 20

## HAZEL

"Hazel, it's two in the morning, what's wrong?"

I hear my dad's low baritone voice, raspier than usual, and I know I've woken him. I can faintly hear my mom's voice, which only means I've awakened her as well and, of course, stirs panic in me.

"Hey, Dad," I say in my best innocent voice. "Why do you assume something is wrong?"

"Because it's two am, and you're calling me, not your irrational mother."

"Um, I may need you to pick us up," I whisper into the phone, hoping my mom can't overhear me talking to my dad, even though that's a totally irrational hope.

"You may need me to pick you up in Texas?" His voice is growing louder and more worried than when he first picked up. "Hazel, where are you? And who is with you?" His tone is sharper than before, and I feel his frustration.

"I'm in jail. In California. With the girls."

"Oh, fuck, Hazel. I'll be there as soon as I can."

"Is it too much to ask you to hurry."

Handcuffed, I walk back to the drunk tank and tell Olivia and Kadin that my dad is on his way to bail us all out. Yep, the three of us have been getting away with far too much shit for our entire lives, and I guess tonight it caught up with us.

"Do you think he's going to tell your mom?" Olivia asks as she tries to get comfortable on the dirty, cold bench we share with several other strangers.

"Of course he will tell my mother why he's leaving the house at two am. If she wakes up and he's gone, she'll have his balls in a blender. Besides, you don't think she wasn't listening to the entire conversation while he was on the phone with me?" The thought of my dad's phone ringing at two am and my mom being okay with it is ridiculous.

Kadin laughs and asks, "Is he going to tell everyone's moms?"

Narrowing my eyes in mock seriousness, I reply, "If I go down, we all go down."

"I didn't even drink!" Olivia exclaims.

"Are you mad?" I ask her.

"Am I mad?" She pauses to choose her words. "Let's just say this isn't how I pictured our first day back in California would end."

"Hey, we're making memories," Kadin says, laughing. Then she lets out a moan and drops her head between her knees.

I lean over to her and quickly pick up her long brown hair from the dirty ground below us.

"I'm sorry, this isn't how I envisioned tonight," I say to Olivia and Kadin.

Olivia rolls her eyes. "It never is, especially when Hayes is involved."

Kadin crosses her arms, her gaze sharp as she looks at me. "Yeah, you two need to figure your shit out!"

I throw my hands up in defense. "This wasn't my fault. Hayes hit Elliot, and I was sticking up for him."

The two of them share a knowing look, and Kadin says, "Yeah, you did, and it pissed off Hayes because he thinks you belong to him."

"Ugh!" I shout.

A drunk lady lifts her head to look at me and then lies back down on the floor.

I continue in a whispered shout, "I don't belong to Hayes."

Olivia says, "Tell him that, because, in his mind, you're his; you've always been his even when you weren't his."

I shake my head. "You're delusional, you know that, right? You both are. And after tonight, Hayes and I are no longer anything, not even friends."

"Just like Jett said at lunch last month, someone would end up in jail if anything happened between you and Hayes. And here we all are sitting in jail at two am. And you can deny you belong to Hayes, but you have always been his girl. Don't you see that, Hazel?" Kadin asks.

"I'm too tired for this right now."

"I'll take that as you understand what I'm saying; you acknowledge what I'm saying, but it's too much to admit your love for Hayes at two a.m.," Kadin says, looking at her watch.

A guard comes and unlocks the door and calls us out one by one by our last names, and I've never sobered up so fast in my entire life. I walk to my dad with my head down, looking at my feet, feeling like a child who just got caught sneaking something she wasn't supposed to have. My dad is standing there, hands in his pocket with an oversized jacket on. The scruff on his face hints he'll need a shave sooner than later. His face falls when he sees us, and I just run over to him, wrap my arms around him, and start to cry. He pulls me into him and says, "Hazel, you're an adult. You don't have to cry to get out of trouble anymore."

"Dad!" I say as I shove myself away from him. Wiping my eyes, I say, "I missed you."

"You just missed the pub more?" he asks, irritated that not only is he bailing us out of jail, but we went to the pub before we went home. Probably not my best decision.

"Ugh, I'll explain later."

He looks past me at Kadin and Olivia and directs them to him with his head. "Hey, girls, you ready to get to bed?"

"Hi, Uncle Gabe," they say in unison, looking at their feet like scolded children.

He gives us a once-over, his lips pressing together. "I'm assuming you ladies are all staying with us tonight."

"Yes!" we all murmur in unison.

As we leave the small police department, Olivia's panic flares up. "What about Jett?" she asks, turning around as if she's going to dash back inside.

"Fuck them," I blurt out, and my dad shoots me a warning glare. I throw up my hands in apology. "Sorry, I've been on my own for a bit."

"Did you turn into a truck driver?" he asks, shaking his head.

"Do you know who raised me? Mom's mouth is worse than mine."

"Can you stay on track for one second?" Olivia interrupts then continues, "We can't leave them here." She takes a deep breath, trying to regain control.

"Calm down, Olivia," my dad says, his voice calm but firm. "I called Hayes's parents; they're on their way if they're not here already."

Just then, the guys walk out of the station, Hayes's mom in tow. Hayes is rubbing his jaw, a small cut on his lip, and

I wonder if it's from me because I don't remember Elliot hitting him.

Olivia immediately hurries across the parking lot to Jett. "Are you okay?" she asks, looking him up and down.

"Yeah, I'm fine," he says, wrapping her in a hug. "Are you okay? How do you feel?" Jett asks her as quietly as he can.

I don't hear her reply or what they say next, but Jett and Olivia turn to look at me, making my skin prickle.

"Don't look at me like that!" I snap. "This is not my fault; it's his," I insist, jabbing a finger at Hayes.

Hayes shakes his head at me, the tiredness in his eyes deep.

His mom turns to him. "Hayes."

He stops her by saying, "Mom, we'll talk about this tomorrow. I just want to get home."

"What's the plan for tomorrow?" Jett asks Olivia. The weight of tonight lingers in this tone.

"You mean today!" Kadin chimes in with a roll of her eyes.

Jett whips his head toward her, irritation flaring in his gaze. "Whatever, Kadin. Why is everyone so pissed at me when I literally did nothing?"

"I'm tired; I'm staying at Hazel's. I'll call you tomorrow," Olivia says, walking toward my dad.

I walk over to Hayes, who's standing by his mom and say to her, "Hello, Mrs. Emerson. It's good to see you. I'm sorry this is the way you're finding out we're home. It was my idea to meet up with our friends from home, but it certainly wasn't my idea for Hayes to hit Elliot in the face and get the cops called on us, getting us all arrested for public intoxication charges."

"I wasn't even drinking!" Olivia shouts from where she's standing with my dad. "I went to jail tonight and didn't even get to enjoy myself. So, if anyone should be pissed, it should be me! Now, let's go home!"

As I turn to walk to my dad, Hayes reaches out to grab my arm. I spin back at him and seethe, "Don't touch me. And don't call me or text me until you apologize to Elliot."

"What about tomorrow?" he asks.

"If you want to be with us tomorrow, you better get your phone out and start groveling."

We get settled into the car and drive out of the crowded parking lot.

"Uncle Gabe," Olivia says, pleading. "Can you not tell my parents before I do? I was hoping you could take me home in the morning and give me an hour or two alone with my parents; then, you could come back with Aunt Harper and Hazel."

In his deep dad's voice, my dad says, "Olivia, you're an adult. I'm not telling your parents anything."

"Does that go for me too?" Kadin asks.

I can't help the chuckle that escapes my mouth. My dad just glares at me.

"Come on, Dad. It's really not my fault, and like you said, *'we're adults'*," I say, still chuckling.

"Maybe you can start asking like an adult," he says, looking at me sidelong.

"Touche, old man." And I give him a nod of approval.

"It's not her fault, Uncle Gabe," Kadin says.

A small smile tugs at my lips, even in this tense situation. I love that she still calls him 'uncle'. It's just a reminder that we'll always be closer than just friends.

"Hayes punched Elliot in the jaw, and someone called the police," Kadin continues.

"Why?" My dad asks, barely taking his eyes off the road.

"Because Elliot offered to drive us to the hotel."

My dad looks at me through the corner of his eye again,

and I see his jaw start to twitch. My dad's jaw twitch is an involuntary tale that he's pissed. He can't control it, no matter how hard he tries.

"Not like that, Dad," I say, disgusted. "But that reminds me." I trail off, rubbing the back of my neck. "We sort of got a hotel for the night, and…um, we need to swing by and grab our suitcases. You know, no big deal or anything."

Kadin shrugs like she's stating the most obvious thing in the world. "You know how Hayes is? He has this thing when guys try to talk to Hazel; he loses his mind and makes really bad decisions."

I glance at my dad, who's been strangely controlled, though there's a glimmer in his eyes like he's enjoying the recap of tonight's chaos a little too much. And then it hits me – those days before we left for college, how dad always trusted Hayes to keep an eye on me. How it felt like he gave him the unspoken job of fending off guys. "Oh my God, Dad!" I interrupt Kadin before I can stop myself. "Did you put him up to this all those years ago when we left for college? Did you make him my official cock blocker?"

"Hazel, I'm too tired for you tonight. Let's just get home and talk about this tomorrow."

# Chapter 21

## OLIVIA

Sleepovers at Hazel's have always been the best because she doesn't have any obnoxious siblings to wake us up early, and today is no different. I open my eyes and check my almost-dead phone. It's 11 am, and my parents have no idea I'm home. I sneak out of Hazel's room and walk down their long hallway to the kitchen. My Aunt Harper has always taken so much pride in her house; it's always clean and free of clutter. The kitchen is a light grey with white cabinets and a huge center island that everyone gathers around when we're here. Fresh flowers are always the centerpiece of her kitchen.

"Good morning," I say to my aunt and uncle, uneasiness creeping in, knowing what today is going to bring. They are sitting side by side at the small breakfast table. My Uncle Gabe always has my Aunt Harper within arm's reach.

"Good morning," my aunt says back to me, motioning me to sit down next to them. "Are you hungry? I can whip up some pancakes," she says with a grin.

I love her famous pancakes.

"Do my parents know I'm here?" I ask, looking between my

aunt and uncle, hoping for some kind of a lifeline.

"I've been instructed to keep my mouth shut," she says, her lips tightening into a thin line as she taps her fingers on the table. "Even though it's killing me to keep a secret like this from your dad," she says with a hint of frustration.

My uncle doesn't even look up. He just keeps eating his eggs like this is the most normal thing in the world.

"I just want you to know I wasn't drinking last night," I add quickly, feeling the need to defend myself.

My aunt takes my hand in hers. "Olivia, your parents and I weren't always old fuddy- duddys. We all have our share of stories." She chuckles softly, her eyes crinkling at the corners. "Did I ever end up in jail? No. But, I never put it past my child to one-up me."

I bite my lip, guilt gnawing at me. "In all honestly, it wasn't her fault. It was Hayes. He hit Elliot when he was only trying to offer a safe ride to our hotel."

"Which brings us to my first and foremost question," she says, still holding my hand, and now I'm wondering if it's so I can't escape.

My uncle looks up, suddenly interested in our conversation. My aunt continues, "One – why are you home two days early, and two – why the secrecy?"

I look down and answer, "That part was my idea. And if it's okay, I'd like to explain myself to you and my parents at the same time."

My aunt nods in understanding and doesn't say another word about it.

"Ugh, I feel like shit!"

I look up to see Hazel leading Kadin down the hallway into the kitchen.

"Well, well, if it isn't my felon daughter and her sidekick."

"Mom, I'm hungover and haven't brushed my teeth yet. Don't make me use my powers for evil."

"You're a heathen, Hazel! What did Texas do to you?" My aunt says as she leans back in her chair, propping one foot under her butt and crossing her arms with a huge grin on her face.

Hazel was afraid her parents would be mad that we didn't tell them we weren't coming home, but they're not. They never got mad at us growing up, rolled with the punches, and never got worked up. So, why would they be mad at us as adults?

Hazel leans over her dad's shoulder and kisses him on top of his head, grabbing his eggs with her fingers.

"Hazel! Get your germ-filled hands out of my food!" he says, pushing her off him. "Did you shower the drunk tank off you, or did you sleep in your filth."

"We slept like this," Kadin answers.

"*Go take a shower now*!" my uncle teases. "Kadin, use Hazel's shower; Hazel, use my shower; and Olivia, dear."

"Olivia, dear," Hazel mimics in a sweet but sarcastic voice that makes me chuckle.

"As I was saying, Olivia, my perfect niece, use the shower upstairs while Harper makes breakfast. Then I'm taking you felons home to your parents before I'm implicated in your crimes."

# Chapter 22

## HAZEL

"Dad, if you kill us because you think staring at me is going to make me talk, you're sadly mistaken." We've just dropped the girls off at their homes, and we're alone for the first time since this whole sorry episode.

"Hazel, what the hell is going on? You do some stupid shit, but this is over-the-top even for you."

I put my head in my hands and groan. "I know, and I promise it'll all make sense in a few hours, but It's not my place to tell you."

"Is Olivia pregnant?"

My head snaps to look at him. "How did you know?"

He looks at me with a shrug and casually says, "I didn't know, but your poker face is worse than your mom's."

"Dad," I protest.

He holds up his hand. "I won't tell your mom, but that still doesn't explain everything."

I look at him, eyes wide. "Since when did you become a detective?"

"I've had free time since you left for college," he deadpans.

"What's going on with Hayes?" he asks, a crease forming on his forehead as he watches me closely, waiting for my answer.

"Dad, I have no fucking clue."

His eyebrows shoot up to his hairline as he says, "Okay, so we're there?"

"Ugh, sorry, but Mom raised me. Blame her," I groan into my hands for the second time today.

"I don't know, Dad. We've accidentally had sex four times in the years we've been away; then he would bring girls back to the house as if I don't exist and just a few weeks ago he told me he wanted to be exclusive. You know, give us a go."

"Didn't need to know all that," he proclaims.

"Dad, I'm going to need you not to be my dad for this or this." I motion between us and continue, "Or, it's never going to work."

He shakes his whole body as if he just stretched out to run a race, and he's getting loose. "Okay, I'm ready. Hit me with it."

"You're so lame, Dad. Have you always been this lame?"

"Yes, your mom tells me all the time. I once was manly and sexy, then I married your her, and now I'm just Harper's husband or Hazel's weird Dad."

I ponder that statement for a minute and pat him on the shoulder. "I'm sorry, Dad. That's terrible, and I never want to get married and have kids now."

This makes him chuckle, and he whispers, "Don't tell your mom I said that."

We pull into the garage and walk into the house together. My mom sits on the couch, one leg bent under her and the other on the floor. Her posture does not hide that she's been there waiting for us to get home. She pats the couch cushion next to her for me to sit down and says, "Do you care to explain anything about the past forty-eight hours to me?"

I meet her gaze, jaw clenched, and my voice comes out sharp. "No," I reply.

She looks at my dad. He shrugs and says, "I'm going to the backyard. I have something to do out there."

"Sit!" my mom orders him.

"I didn't get arrested last night; why am I in trouble?"

"Because I know you know something that you're not telling me, and one of you two is going to come clean."

Being raised with no siblings has always made me the main character, so I've embraced my role in life. My mom and dad were helicopter parents growing up; and they still are.

It's terrifying to witness the slow morph into your parents. It doesn't hit you all at once. One day, you wake up, and voila, you're them. I've always been a spitting image of my mom – exactly like her. But she's reserved, while I'm the life of the party. Her favorite color is black; mine is pink. She never cries; I cry at the drop of a hat. My love language is physical touch, while her love language isn't even an option in that famous book everyone talks about in my human services class.

My dad, on the other hand, is the most emotional man you'll ever meet. Not in a crying way, but she is hot one minute and then cold the next. He has a literal switch. Tell him that fact, and you can watch him in real-time. And that twitch in his jaw; it's his tell. He can't hide it.

My parents love each other dearly; they're best friends. It's annoying. Do you know how hard it is to have a relationship when your dad always judges your boyfriend and your mom tells you to make sure there are sparks and chemistry? Without that, dating isn't worth it. But then, in the same breath, telling you not to have sex with just anyone because 'you give away a part of yourself with every sexual experience'. *Like, what the hell? Pick a side, Mom.* Do you want me to find the one, or do you want me to save myself for the one? I just realize that maybe it's possible to do both. I ponder that possibility for a minute.

I take a deep breath and sink onto the couch.

"Mom, there's not a lot to say. Olivia needed to come home early, and she didn't want to tell her parents because they'd be concerned, so… Surprise! I'm home."

My phone vibrates with a call, pulling my attention from the conversation with my parents. I look at the screen, and it's a picture of Hayes and me singing karaoke at a bar from a year ago when I thought maybe that would be the turning point. Spoiler alert: it wasn't.

"I'm going to take this to my room!" I announce, sprinting up the stairs two at a time. "My room," I repeat, glancing back at my mom with an exaggerated hand over my heart, feigning nostalgia. "Ah, the sanctuary of my teenage angst and endless daydreams."

Mom rolls her eyes, a smile tugging at the corners of her lips. "Just don't trip over those dreams on your way up," she teases, shaking her head.

"Too late!" I call back, laughing as I narrowly avoid a step, my hand clutching the railing for dear life. "But don't worry, I think I left some dignity under my bed!"

As I reach the top, I pause for a second, take a deep breath, and look around. The familiar creak of the floorboards and the posters of old bands on the walls bring a flood of memories.

"What do you want?" I answer Hayes's incoming call.

"Good morning to you."

"I told you I'm not talking to you."

"I called Elliot this morning. We're cool."

"Good, so why are you calling me?"

"I need to see you."

I lie back on my bed and stare up at the same ceiling. I've searched for answers so many times after hanging up with Hayes over the years.

"Hayes, I really don't have the mental capacity for the *'you and me'* drama today. I have so much to deal with. Why do you insist on making today harder?"

"Hazel, I just want to be there for you today." His words should surprise me, but they don't. Hayes has always been there for me—every breakup, most of which he caused, every birthday, every dance competition. He's always been an integral part of my life.

I sigh, the weight of his truth both comforting and exhausting. "You've always been there, Hayes," I murmur, my voice tinged with a mixture of gratitude and frustration. "But sometimes, I need space to breathe, to figure things out without you."

The ceiling blurs as memories flood my mind, of every moment he's been by my side, every instance he's added to the chaos of my heart. I turn my head to the side, glancing at the photos on my dresser, reminders of our tumultuous history. "Today is about Olivia, Hayes. I need you to respect that."

He's silent for a moment, and I can almost hear the gears turning in his mind.

"Alright," he finally says, his voice softer and almost resigned. "I'll give you space. But remember, I'm here if you need me."

I close my eyes, taking a deep breath. "I know," I whisper, more to myself than to him. "I know."

# Chapter 23

## OLIVIA

"Olivia, is that you?" she asks. Her voice is soft and warm.

"Yes, it's me."

"You look just like your Mom. I miss her so much," she says as she wraps herself around me. She's so warm.

"Am I dead?" I ask as I look around.

"No, dear, you're not dead. You're dreaming."

"Great-Grandma, I'm dying, and my mom will never be okay again..."

The ringing of my phone threatens to rob me of my dream, but I fight to stay rooted there. I'm pleading with someone I've never met.

"Don't leave me yet. I'm not done talking to you. Will you be here waiting for me?"

"Olivia." My mom shakes me awake.

"What... Where am I?" I ask as I sit up on the couch at my parents' house.

"Are you okay, Olivia? You were having a bad dream. I could hear you shouting from down the hall."

Taking a deep breath, knowing I can't keep this secret from my parents any longer, I finally surrender to my mom and say, "Mom, I need to talk to you and Dad."

"Is everything Okay, Olivia? What is going on? You're scaring me." Her hands are balled into fists, knuckles white, and her usually calm, steady voice wavers just slightly, as if her motherly intuition has told her something I've been too scared to tell her.

"Is this why you guys are home early? Is this why you've been avoiding my calls?" She panics, just as I knew she would.

There was zero chance we'd have a rational conversation about this in a few hours.

I quickly grab my cell phone from the bedside and text Hazel without answering my mom's questions.

*Me* – It's time.

*Hazel* – We'll be there in 10 minutes.

"Olivia!" my mom shouts. "What is going on? I'm trying to talk to you, and you are texting?"

"Mom, give me ten minutes to wake up. I had a long night. I'll meet you and Dad in the kitchen."

*Me* – HURRY UP

*Hazel* – Getting in the car now.

Five minutes later, I'm walking to the family room. I pass my brothers on the stairs, both of them absorbed in a video game.

"You're better off staying up here," I say quietly, leaning toward them. "I'll fill you in later."

They both give me a brief nod without pausing their game.

I take a seat on my favorite armchair in the family room. My dad sits, looking confused, watching my mom pace the floor. There's a knock at the door.

"I'll get it," I say as I rush down the hallway to greet my Aunt Harper, Uncle Gabe, Hazel, and Jett.

"What's going on, Olivia?" My mom's voice cracks, her desperation palpable as she stops pacing long enough to lock her eyes on me, pleading for answers.

My aunt and uncle hug my mom and dad and then awkwardly mill around the living room, trying to blend in with the furniture.

"Harper, do you know what's going on?" my dad asks, his voice tinged with worry.

My aunt looks down at her feet, avoiding my dad's eye. She moves slowly and sits beside him, placing a comforting hand on his leg. My Uncle Gabe sits next to her, and Hazel sits on the arm of the couch by her dad.

I stay standing, Jett by my side, though I feel the weight of his silent concern.

"Mom, sit down by Dad." I say, my voice calmer than I expect.

Without protest, my mom crosses the room, her movements deliberate, as though bracing her impact. She sits on the opposite side of my aunt, waiting for the words she already senses will change everything.

"Olivia, what's going on?" My dad's voice cuts through the silence, sharper now.

I take a deep, calming breath, bracing myself for the most challenging conversation of my life. What I'm about to share with my parents will shatter their hearts. My thoughts are a chaotic mess, just like my emotions right now. But they need to hear it all, no matter how jumbled my words might be.

"Mom, Dad, I dropped out of school about three weeks ago."

My mom immediately starts to cry, knowing I wouldn't call everyone here to tell them I dropped out of school, her intuition telling her there's more to my confession.

"Olivia, what the hell is going on?" My dad interrupts, irritation evident in his voice.

Jett takes my hand in his and nods, giving me the courage I need to continue.

"Mom, Dad, early on in my senior year, I started getting sick every morning at school," I begin, my voice wavering slightly. "I had Hazel take me to the doctor." I pause, glancing between them, then add, "Actually, now that I think back, I was missing a few activities even during junior year. I just assumed it was stress from school or all the pressure building up."

"Are you pregnant, Olivia?" Mom interrupts, her hands slapping down on her knees with a mix of determination and worry. She looks at me with resolve; her opinion on what needs to happen is already formed. "If you're pregnant, we can handle this. We'll deal with it together."

"Oh my God," My Aunt Harper says, touching her heart. "You're pregnant, Olivia?"

"I am pregnant, and I'm so excited about it. I didn't think I'd be this excited, but I lay in bed at night, completely still trying to feel it kick and daydreaming about meeting him or her."

My mom turns to Jett, her gaze sharp with a question that catches me off guard. "How do you feel about this?" she asks.

She didn't even know about us until right now; I hadn't expected her to be so composed.

"I'm so excited to meet our baby. I'm in this with Olivia, Mrs. Barlow."

"What about football?" My dad asks Jett.

"It's the off-season, sir. Olivia and I will cross that bridge when and if I'm drafted."

"I think we got sidetracked," I say and quickly continue before my parents can continue to interrogate Jett. And before I lose my nerve.

"When I say I was ill, I was very ill. I couldn't eat, and when I did, I would vomit profusely. I was losing weight, and I would sleep all day. I was missing class, and my grades were suffering. So, we went back to the doctor, and they did every blood test imaginable." My eyes fill with tears as I once again look at Hazel. It would be so much easier if she could tell our parents, but I know that's not an option.

I continue after a deep inhale, "Mom, Dad, I have stage four brain cancer."

My mom jumps up from the couch, her hands flying to her mouth as if trying to hold in the panic bubbling up. "Stop it, Olivia, you do not have cancer. This is crazy." Her voice shakes, louder than usual, betraying the fear that's quickly swallowing her. She looks at my dad, her eyes wide and desperate, pleading for some rationality.

"Xavier, tells her this is crazy." She's pacing, her movements erratic, as if movement will make my confession disappear.

I've seen hundreds of movies in my life, and I've always wondered if people overacted when faced with devastating news. Today, I'm living one of those scenes, and I say from first-hand experience not one actor or actress ever overacted. If anything, they didn't do the scene justice.

Tears well up in my dad's eyes. The man who always has a plan, always knows what to do, is now grasping at straws, desperate for a lifeline that doesn't exist. The pain in his expression mirrors my own, and for a moment, it feels like we're both falling into an abyss with no way to stop the descent.

My Aunt Harper grips my dad's leg, and my uncle puts his arm around her as if preparing for something much bigger.

"No, no, no, no, no, no, no. This is not real; this is not happening." My Mom paces in front of everyone, repeatedly chanting the word 'no'.

"Mom," I say, and everyone's eyes are on me again, but before I can say anything more, my dad stands up and walks over to me. He wraps me in a hug as if we are the only two people in the room. I feel his body convulsing; silent sobs engulf the air around us.

My Uncle Gabe rises from his seat and says, "We should go."

"No, don't go, please stay," I beg, my voice cracking.

My Aunt Harper stands slowly, her eyes filled with unshed tears as she walks toward me. Without a word, she wraps me in a warm embrace, pressing a gentle kiss to my temple just like she used to when I was a kid.

She pulls back slightly, her hands resting on my shoulders for a minute before taking Hazel's hand, and leading her family out of the front door, leaving me alone with my parents and Jett.

My dad puts some distance between us and says, "What is happening, Olivia? Why are we just hearing about this?"

I continue, "Looking back on my decision now, it wasn't the correct one, and I'm sorry. I found out I was pregnant at twelve weeks. I was just going to finish college in Texas and then obviously move back home or to wherever Jett got drafted. It was simple. It was exciting, actually. I was going to tell you in person, maybe schedule a fight out here and surprise you, but then, two weeks later, I found out I was dying, and that's not a conversation you have over FaceTime. Could you imagine if I called with this news?"

"You're not dying, Olivia," my mom shouts at me. "We will

beat whatever this is."

I lower my voice. "No, Mom, *we* won't. The survival rate of this type of cancer is near impossible and will require chemo and radiation, which will put the baby in jeopardy. I'm not risking my baby's life so I can live."

Jett, still silent, looks down to his feet, and tears fall to his shoes. I take his hand.

"This is fucking crazy," my mom screams, clearly out of control.

My dad silently holds her.

"Olivia, if you think we aren't fighting this, you're wrong," my mom says, insistent.

"Mom, if there's a chance for survival after I have this baby, I will allow you to make my final days here on earth torture with chemo and radiation, but there is no way I'll consider anything other than natural remedies until then."

"So, you're going to have a baby and then die? What then, Olivia? Have you thought any of this through?" my mom yells, her arms flailing wildly. She's beyond furious; in fact, furious doesn't even begin to describe the intensity of her emotions.

"Jett and I are getting married," I blurt out before I can stop myself.

My dad whips his head in my direction, his eyes wide with disbelief. "*What*, Olivia, you're a child!"

Tears prick the back of my eyes as I stand a little straighter, forcing myself to meet his gaze. "I'm dying, and I'd like to have my dad walk me down the aisle before I die."

As realization sets in, a heavy silence blankets the room.

# Chapter 24

## HAZEL

The drive home is quiet. I sit in the backseat, the world outside blurring as houses and trees rush by, a stark contrast to the turmoil churning in my chest. My dad grips the wheel tightly, eyes fixed on the road, while my mom sits beside him, her fingers drumming nervously on her thigh.

Unable to stand the silence – because my mom has never felt at ease with it – she turns slightly, and says, "Hazel, in what universe do you and your cousin live in that you thought it would be a good idea to keep this from us for a day, let alone six weeks? Do you know the help we could've gotten Olivia in the last six weeks? This is time we cannot get back, each minute passing quicker than the one before."

"Mom, I know we are your children, but I am not a child anymore. I'm twenty-two, and I can make my own decisions. Do you think I'm okay knowing my cousin is dying and is refusing to undergo any form of treatment because it can potentially hurt her unborn child? Do you think I want to drop out of school and move home with you and Dad so my entire focus in life can be spending as much time with Olivia as possible before she dies? Do you think I want to have kids without Olivia?"

Tears stream down my face, but my determination to tell my mom exactly how I feel is not wavering. "Do you think I want her death to define me as your cousin, did you?"

My Mom starts to say something, but I put my hand up. "Please, Mom. Jett, Olivia, and I have been going back and forth for weeks trying to convince her to seek treatment. She refuses. Treatment for this type of tumor will add maybe a year to her life, but the fucked reality is no matter how aggressive they are, she is still going to die, so why should she kill her unborn child with her? She's literally making the ultimate sacrifice for her baby, and no *child* would do that, so please stop treating her like one. Stop treating her like she doesn't have a say about the shitty circumstances she was dealt. I get to say goodbye to her. I get to hold her hand when she leaves this earth. My only hope is that her baby will be born healthy before that happens. So, for the next however long, I am going to be strong and do whatever she needs from me. Then, when the time comes, I will hide in my bedroom, mourn the loss of not only my cousin but my best friend, then I will pick myself up and continue to live just a little less happy, knowing I'll never hear Olivia's laugh ever again."

We pull into the driveway, and my dad kills the engine, but no one moves, no one says anything. We sit there for a minute longer, each of us lost in what I just said. Finally, my dad unbuckles his seatbelt and opens the door with a sigh. "Let's go inside," he mutters.

My mom hesitates, wiping he eyes quickly before stepping out of the car. She walks around to my side, opening the door. I look up at her as she extends her hand to help me out, her touch soft and comforting.

I get out but linger for a minute, leaning against the car. I let myself breathe in the stillness for the first time in what feels like days. My parents slowly make their way toward the house. My mom pauses, turning back. She steps toward me, wrapping her arms around me in a warm, familiar embrace. "I love you," she whispers, her voice steady.

I nod, squeezing her back tightly and grounding myself in her embrace. When she lets go, she follows my dad toward the house. Just as they reach the door, my dad glances back, his voice is soft. "Are you coming?"

"No," I reply. "I'm going to take a walk."

He hesitates for a second, and then my mom speaks up, her eyes searching mine. "Are you sure? Do you want me to come?"

"Mom," I sigh, a small smile tugs at my lips. "Dad bailed me out of jail yesterday, so I think I'll be okay taking a walk. I haven't been alone in a long time and just need some fresh air."

They exchange a glance before my dad pulls her under his arm, holding her close. As they step inside, I watch as my mom buries her face into his chest, her shoulders trembling softly. I know, even without hearing her, that she's scared – scared not only for Olivia but reliving the pain of her own cousin's death from years ago.

I take a deep breath, pulling out my phone. The screen glows softly as I start a text to Olivia:

*Me* – How are they?

*Olivia* – In denial

*Me* – Do you blame them? We've known for six weeks.

*Olivia* – No, I don't blame them, but it doesn't make it any easier to convince your parents to be happy about your unplanned pregnancy and accept the fact that you refuse to be a lab rat the last year of your life.

*Me* – Yeah, I guess give your mom a break, okay?

*Me* – Did you tell Nolen and Jensen?

*Olivia* – They heard, how could they not? I feel like the entire street heard.

*Me* – I just assumed they had their game headsets on.

*Olivia* – Nope

*Me* – How are they?

*Olivia* – Quiet.

Even though we're just texting, I can sense the weight she's carrying. Jensen and Nolen are inseparable, and even though there are a few years between her and the boys, Olivia's always felt a sense of responsibility toward them, like she's their anchor, even when they don't realize it.

Bubbles appear and then disappear, so I lock my phone and stuff it in the pocket of my shorts. I continue to walk along my street, making a left before the dead end, and aimlessly continue along the single lane just off the main road. The path is flanked by dirt and colorful weeds. The sun is sitting high in the sky, barely visible. A scattering of clouds lazily hangs over the hills far in the distance, casting shadows. The California sun is softer in a way that Texas could never replicate. I didn't realize how much I missed it until now, its glow touching everything in its path, including the man up in front of me, leaning casually against his car. With one leg nonchalantly extended, he exudes an air of relaxation as he patiently waits for me. As I walk toward him, I feel an unexpected sense of ease as he looks at me and watches me as I approach.

"Hayes, what are you doing here? How did you even know where to find me? I'm still not talking to you."

"Hazel, I've watched you walk down this road every time you've been in trouble at school or at home. I chased you down this street when we were kids, and I've followed you down this street every time I hurt you in high school." His voice is hushed as he pulls me into him. "Are you okay?"

"No," I answer him honestly. "I don't think I'll ever be okay again, Hayes. My cousin is dying, which is going to kill her parents; I'm dropping out of school; you beat up Elliot. I think I hate you, and now I'm home with my parents."

I pull away and continue. "Growing up, did you ever imagine what your future would look like?"

"Yes, Hazel, I did, and I would be playing professional football if my childhood dreams came true."

"No, Hayes, not dreams, but visions. Visions that unfold like movies where you can see and hear everything that is happening around you. Visions that you can feel here," I say as I put my hand over his heart. "We did. We envisioned our weddings; we envisioned raising our kids together like our parents, and we envisioned family vacations and weekend barbeques. Olivia dying from cancer wasn't part of those movies."

"You can still have all those things. You don't have to give up the hope of having Olivia in your life because she'll live on through the baby. Between Jett, Kadin, you, and me, do you think we'll ever let the memory of Olivia die?"

"Today, right now, is a turning point in all our lives, and I feel like I'm the only one who is grasping the magnitude of what's next."

"Hazel," he says, his voice tender as he gently tilts my chin to meet his gaze. "There will never be another girl for me. You've been my girl since we were kids. It's always been you. I've spent the last four years in college surrounded by countless girls, and none of them compared to you. You're the only girl I want to marry; you're the only girl I've ever wanted to marry."

"Why are you saying this right now?" I shake my head in disbelief.

"I know this is terrible timing." His eyes fix on mine. "I'll never forget what your Dad told me all those years ago, after that dance when Elliot and I got in a fight over you. He said, 'If you have the right girl, then there isn't a wrong time.' I'm finally taking his advice. Marry me, Hazel."

"What, *no*!" I shout. "Marry you?" I just told you minutes ago I hated you, and now, after all these years, you have chosen to ask me to marry you. Are you insane? We just started officially dating, and we've accidentally only had sex four times, three of which I don't even remember if you were any good!"

That causes him to chuckle, and he says, "Hazel, not one of those times was an accident. All four were amazing, and you've always been my girl; you just wouldn't admit it to yourself."

"You're crazy, Hayes."

"Yep, you make me crazy. You make me crazy when you talk to other guys, you make me crazy when you avoid me, and you make me crazy when you don't."

His words sink in, and the pain in my chest is unbearable. "I'm not going to marry you!" I insist.

"Let me into your life completely; let me be the husband you deserve; let me prove to you that we can be as happy as your parents. Let me comfort you through what will be the hardest year of our lives. Then, we'll finish college together; we'll support Jett in raising Olivia and his baby. If you want Olivia to be your maid of honor, I'll marry you tomorrow; if you need time to process and have something good to look forward to, then I'll wait for you. I've been waiting for you for fifteen years; what's another year or two?"

At that moment, with Olivia's illness, the baby, and our family's uncertainty, I find clarity in his words. Tears pull in my eyes, and I throw my arms around him and whisper into his chest, "Maybe, Hayes, maybe I will marry you, but not now."

"What do you mean, not now?"

"We need to continue dating first; we need to let Olivia and Jett to take center stage until we have to say goodbye to her."

"Okay," he says, pushing a loose strand of hair behind my ear. But we don't need to date, Hazel. I know everything about you, and you know me. I know your heart, and it's home for me."

"Hayes, I'm serious. No ring, no nothing."

"Can we kiss?"

I push his chest and say, "You're so weird."

"Is that a yes?"

I pull his face down to mine and say, "Of course, it's a yes. Now shut up and kiss me before I change my mind."

# Chapter 25

## OLIVIA

After jumping from my bed, I throw my bedroom door open and run into the bathroom I share with Nolen and Jensen. I drop to my knees and start to vomit uncontrollably into the pee-stained toilet. I hear my mom run down the hall and throw one of my brothers against a wall.

"Ouch, Mom," he whines, and it's hard for me not to laugh.

Mom drops down behind me, scooping my hair into a ponytail and wrapping it securely in a scrunchie she had around her wrist.

"Are you okay?" she asks softly, her hand lingering on my shoulder after finishing my hair.

"Other than my cancer-ridden brain and my body protesting this pregnancy, I'm great," I try for humor, but it falls flat.

"Olivia, be serious. How can I help?" She kneels beside me now, her eyes searching mine.

"You can help me by making the boys use your bathroom, and you and I can share this one. The boys have terrible aim, and I'm hovering over this toilet more than I'm sitting upright."

"Okay, I'll talk to Dad."

"I'd also like Jett to move in here until..." I stop only to spare my mom's emotions.

Her eyes are swollen, and the purple bags and a few new wrinkles are a sign of how hard these last few days have been on her.

"Okay, I'll talk to Dad," she repeats her earlier response.

I turn to face her, trying to lighten the mood. "You and I need to get massages once a week; they say it's good for the cancer." I laugh, and Mom rests her back against the cabinets.

"Mom, please." I stop, as the words get stuck in my throat. What do I even say to her?

"It's not fair," Mom says in a whisper, looking away as her voice cracks.

"You're telling me. We used protection and everything." I nudge her shoulder playfully, trying to break through the sadness.

She gives me a small, sad smile and asks, "Olivia, are you ever serious?"

"Nope, not anymore," I reply with a shrug. "Life is too short to be serious."

She gives me a side-eye.

I shrug and continue, "I'd like Aunt Harper, Hazel, Kadin, and Aunt Roxy to dress shop with us today. Is that okay?"

Her hand squeezes mine gently. "I wouldn't have it any other way."

I nod in agreement as tears blur my vision. Trying to steady my voice, I whisper, "I love you, Mom, and I'm sorry for leaving you like everyone else did when you were a child. But you'll still have Dad and the twins. And I'll finally get to meet your grandma."

Another wave of emotion floods me at the mention of the grandmother that I've only known through stories. I confess,

"I think she comes to me often in my dreams now. She says she is waiting for me, and I believe her."

As the weight of the inevitable hangs between Mom and me, tears flow down both our faces as I continue, "I know that my last breath here with you will be my first breath with her. I'm leaving you with my baby, so every time you look at her, you'll see me."

A choked sob escapes my mom's lips as she pulls me closer to her.

"Mom, no matter what treatment we try, I'm going to die. I'm willing to take six months off my life for my baby."

My mom looks at me with unbearable pain in her eyes. "You said her, you said when you look at her." Her voice cracks, barely holding herself together. "I can't lose you for her."

• • •

As I glance around the parking lot, I spot Aunt Roxanne leaning against her car with Kadin, her excitement clear in the way her foot taps against the pavement. My Aunt Harper stands nearby, arms folded watching everyone with her quiet composure as Hazel, who is the exact opposite of her, dances in the middle of our cars to whatever tune is playing on repeat in her head.

We're at the same dress shop where my Aunt Roxanne got her wedding dress. It's a pristine white building with a massive double-door entry and a gold sign that *reads 'The Blushing Bride'*. As we approach the building, the four mannequins in the windows come into focus, all adorned in elaborately beaded dresses in different shades of white and creams.

I look back to my mom and Aunt Roxanne, who are holding hands so tightly that their knuckles are white, and I say, "Does this bring back memories?"

My mom smiles. "Oh, you have no idea. We went dress shopping the day of my birthday. I never used to celebrate my birthday. Long story, one for another day."

We all turn to look at her.

She raises a dismissive hand and says, "Like I said, long story. Anyway, your dad took us to the fanciest restaurant in Los Angeles, and I made a fool of myself."

I can see my Aunt Roxanne laughing now, so I insist, "Aunt Roxy, tell us everything."

"Your mom was throwing an absolute fit about the fact that your dad was taking us out to dinner. She failed to tell him she didn't like to celebrate her birthday, so we basically lied to him all night. Your mom then proceeded to accost a poor young waiter, making him spill his water glasses all down the front of her. She panicked and ran to the restroom."

My mom interrupts, "I was soaked! I had to slick back my hair in a tight pony and try to embrace the look. Your Aunt Roxy wouldn't stop laughing at me, which only added to my fury. It was terrible!"

My Aunt Roxanne interjects, "It wasn't terrible. We ended up having a great time, and that was the last birthday your mom didn't celebrate her birthday."

● ● ●

Stepping out of the dressing room, I'm wearing a champagne-colored dress that complements my hair color. Its low-cut front shows off a satin bodice and is elegantly backless. The empire waist offers adjustability that I may need to accommodate my growing baby. But the star of the show is the layers upon layers of tulle. There's a delicate touch of beading on the skirt that adds the perfect amount of sparkle. The second I put it on, I knew it was the one.

My Aunt Harper is the first one to gasp when she catches sight of me, while Kadin does this loud whistle that she obviously learned on the soccer field. Hazel nudges her playfully, shaking her head in amusement. My mom stands, taking my arm. With a proud smile, she lifts my arm above my head, twirling me around to admire the dress from every angle, watching the skirt dance gracefully around me as I spin.

"Mom, I'm pregnant and dying; you can't keep spinning me or I'll throw up."

Clearly lost in the moment, she says, "Oh God, I'm sorry, babe. You look perfect."

# Chapter 26

## OLIVIA

Hazel, Kadin, Jett, and all our moms are once again together, however this time we're crammed into the very small examination room at my doctor's office. When the door opens, the doctor steps in, her eyes widening in surprise as she looks around the crowded room. She pauses mid-step, blinking. "Oh," she says, placing her hand on her chest. "It's a party in here."

My mom immediately reaches out her hand to shake the doctors.

"Hello, I'm Joy. I'm Olivia's mom."

Dr. Smith is young, maybe in her early thirties, with thick, long, natural black hair that shines under all the lights in the office. Her petite stature gets eaten up by the number of people in the room. Dr. Smith nods at my mom, then walks over to Jett and says, "I'm assuming you're Dad?"

He clears his throat. "Yes, ma'am, I am. I'm Jett."

"Okay, Jett, I'm going to need you right here by Mom's head."

I immediately start crying, my breath hitching as I try to hold back sobs. The room goes still, my shifts in her seat, her eyes wide with worry as she looks between Jett and me. Hazel moves closer, but instinctively, my Aunt Harper, calm and controlled, grabs her arm to root her in place.

"What's wrong?" Jett whispers in my ear.

"Mom—no one has ever called me that before." My voice quivers as I turn to Jett, tears welling up in my eyes. "Jett, I'm a mom." The words feel both foreign and deeply profound, echoing through the room.

He kisses my forehead, wipes a few tears that escaped, and says, "You're going to be the best mom ever, Olivia."

Dr. Smith walks to my side, pulls up a saddle chair on wheels, and proceeds to talk to only Jett and me. "Are we finding out the sex of the baby today?"

"Yes," we both answer together.

"Okay then. I know you're aware, Olivia, that everyone in this room is going to be privy to everything we talk about in here. Are you okay with that?"

"Yes, they're all my family," I say, looking around the room.

"Jett, are you comfortable being the only man in a room full of women?"

He chuckles and says, "Story of my life, doctor."

"Okay, then we'll proceed. Olivia, when was your last appointment with your neurologist?"

"It was back in Texas; my mom has been looking for one here."

Looking back to my mom, she says, "I'm going to need you to speed up the process, Mom."

My mom stays silent and nods at her while my Aunt Roxanne pulls her into a side hug.

"Okay," my doctor claps her hands together, says, "Let's get this show started. According to what your first doctor sent over you should be twenty weeks."

The same whooshing sound that Hazel and I experienced when I was only 12 weeks pregnant fills the room once again. Jett's hand finds mine, and his grip tightens, a silent acknowledgment that this is the first time he's hearing our baby's heartbeat. I steal this moment for myself, closing my eyes to silence the gasps and chatter of my mom, my aunts, and my best friends. This moment is reserved for Jett, the baby, and me.

Jett's grip on my hand tightens, and I open my eyes to see the image of our baby on the monitor. My mom's sobs harmonize with the whooshing noise. Jett's mom is quiet as silent tears escape her eyes. My Aunt Harper wraps Hazel and Kadin in each of her arms while my Aunt Roxanne tends to my mom.

Dr. Smith looks between Jett and me and asks, "Are we ready?"

Jett and I nod in agreement, and she whispers, so only Jett and I can hear, "It's a healthy baby girl."

I let out a huge sigh of relief. I knew it was a girl this whole time. I hoped for a girl, not for myself, but for my mom. She will need a reminder of me. This baby girl will be her way of holding onto me forever. My mom deserves for this baby to be a girl. "I knew she was a girl," I whisper to Jett as he places his forehead on mine.

• • •

On the way home, we stop at the bakery for our big gender reveal cake. It's round, made of very pastel blue fondant. The top of the cake is covered in blush-pink frosting that drips down the sides. White edible flowers frame a gold sign that reads 'Oh Baby' on top. Under all that frosting, there are three layers: one pink layer sandwiched between white cake.

I silently watch a girl about my age behind the counter,

carefully placing my cake in a box, She's bright-eyed, carefree with her whole life ahead of her. I watch her hands move methodically, making sure not to smear the frosting. I can't help but feel the weight of everything I'm going to miss out on. A knot tightens in my chest as I realize how young she looks—how young I am. Too young to have a child, too young to get married, and definitely too young to die.

"Are you okay?" my mom asks, her voice pulling me from my thoughts. "You've been quiet."

I lean against the counter, still watching the girl behind it, wondering what her life will look like in the next few years. Will she get married? Travel? Live her dreams? A pang of envy stirs inside me. "Yes, I'm fine, just a little tired."

"Do you want me to cancel tonight?" she asks.

"No, please don't," I say, shaking my head. "Are you sure you're okay with Jett moving in after we get married this weekend?"

"Olivia, there's a lot I'm not okay with in life right now, but watching you marry Jett and him moving in here isn't one of them. I understand," she says, reassuring me.

"What else is on your mind?" she asks, and it occurs to me that my mom never really asks so many questions.

"Nothing," I lie. But, I'm tired of hiding stuff from my mom, so I admit, "I can't stop asking myself if I want Jett to fall in love again after I die. I do; I truly want Jett to fall in love and move forward. But do I want someone raising my daughter beside me? No. I don't. But, if I'm being honest, I wish I wasn't dying yet; here we are."

"I'm sorry, Olivia."

"No, mom. I'm sorry. When I'm dead, I'm dead, but you'll be left here to deal with the heartache, and I'm so sorry for that."

"Have you and Jett thought of any names for the baby?"

she asks, clearly trying to change the subject.

"Yes, we are naming her May," I say as I look to my mom for her reaction.

May is my mom's middle name, as is mine. Yep, my parents named me Olivia May Barlow. You'd think I was raised on a farm instead of a few miles outside of Los Angeles.

"May is a great name, babe," she says, wiping a stray tear from her cheek.

"I thought so, too." I give her a knowing smile.

As soon as my mom and I pull into the driveway, I can see the house is already buzzing. Cars line our street. We step out of the car, and I hold the cake box carefully as we make our way up to the door. Before I can even reach for the handle, Jett swings it open, his face lighting up. "Let me help with that," he says, taking the cake from my hands and giving me a quick kiss on my cheek.

Inside the house, there is conversation and laughter. The smell of food – probably Aunt Roxanne's famous casserole – wafts through the air. Plates and appetizers are already set out on the kitchen island.

Jett carries the cake into the kitchen, where the majority of our guests are gathered. My dad notices us walk in and, unable to hide his impatience, asks, "Are you going to make us wait?"

I grin and shake my head. "No, not too long."

I say hello to a few of my parents' friends, most I haven't seen since I left for college, then quickly move to the couch where Hayes and Hazel sit, practically glowing with their not-so-hidden feelings for each other.

I look around the room for Kadin, but she's nowhere in sight.

"Where's Kadin?" I ask Hazel.

She shrugs, brows knitting together as she glances around. "I don't know. Haven't seen her since the sonogram."

Part of me feels relieved she's not here. Every time, I see her, a knot tightens in my chest. The guilt almost unbearable. I stole the love of her life, made her drop out of college and skip the remainder of her soccer season. I know she's pissed at me, but she'll never admit it.

My mom calls me to the kitchen and hands Jett and me a big knife and nods, giving us the universal sign for 'go ahead'. Jett and I hold the handle together, and we cut into the cake, revealing a single layer of pink cake sandwiched between the two white layers.

"It's a girl!" Nolen exclaims from behind me, and the room erupts in cheers.

"What's her name?" my dad asks.

I look to Jett and then to my dad and say, "Her name is May."

# Chapter 27

## HARPER

*Harper –* How are you holding up?

*Xavier –* I'm not sure I even know how I'm functioning anymore.

*Harper –* Drinks tonight

*Xavier –* I've been waiting for you to ask me.

*Harper –* I hope that's not true.

*Xavier –* It is, but yes. Drinks tonight.

*Xavier –* Just you and I, correct?

*Xavier –* I just need a second to myself.

*Harper –* I wouldn't want it any other way.

"Seriously! You guys are going to dinner and Top-Putt the one night I'm going out with Xavier?"

"Don't be a baby, Harper; I haven't seen Hazel since she's been home, and you guys have been together every day."

"You bailed her out of jail."

Gabe leans back, crossing his arms with a smirk "Oh yes, quality time spent," he says as he rolls his eyes.

"Dad, is it okay if Hayes tags along?" Hazel yells from downstairs.

I bat my eyelashes at Gabe as he rolls his eyes at me yet again. Deep down, I know Hazel and Hayes will end up together. He loves her, but he's a boy. I've watched him watch her since they were in elementary school. I watched him as he walked extra slow past our house, hoping she'd be outside with the girls. I watched him follow her home from school. I watched him watch her when she'd talk to other boys growing up.

"Say yes!" I whisper shout at him. "It's fine," I yell down to her without giving Gabe an opportunity to protest. "Something is going on with them. I can feel it."

"Your motherly instincts are running overtime; give it a rest. She can make her own decisions. Get off her about Hayes."

"I will do no such thing," I say before I kiss him on the cheek and turn to head downstairs.

"You look amazing," Gabe says to me. "Are you sure you're up to this? I have a terrible feeling you're going to drink yourself into oblivion and not be able to function for a few days. We have the wedding reception here at our house this weekend."

"I'm fine, babe," I say as I make my way back to him and wrap my arms around his waist. Tonight isn't for me; it's for Xavier."

"I know, but that's never stopped you from indulging too much in the past."

We walk down the stairs together, and Hazel is standing there at the bottom, looking up at us.

"Hot date with Uncle Xavier?"

"Just like old times before your old dad here tied me down."

Gabe just laughs at my comment.

"Mom, you better not call here at 2 a.m. looking to get picked up from jail."

Again, Gabe laughs, but just a little bit harder at her joke than mine, and a flurry of emotions overtakes me as I think about how thankful I am for my family, while feeling such sorrow for Olivia.

• • •

## XAVIER

"Joy, are you fine if I head out to meet Harper?"

"Yes, but are you going you going to stay out all night and come home drunk?"

"I hope so!" I shout back to her, and I can hear her laugh from the hall. The sound takes me back to a simpler time when my daughter wasn't pregnant and before I knew she was dying.

"Dad, I'm sleeping with Mom tonight, so you can sleep in my room when you get home."

"Sleepover!" I hear Joy scream from our bedroom.

Chuckling, I grab my keys from the kitchen counter. "Good night, everyone! Don't wait up!" I shout over my shoulder.

I back out of the garage and drive the familiar route to my favorite bar. My mood lifts even more as I see the neon sign come into view. Harper and I have been meeting here for years—long before she married Gabe, before I had kids, and before my life imploded just a few short weeks ago.

Walking in, I look around for Harper. She waves from a table in the bar area. I walk over to her, and she stands to hug me.

"How are you?" she asks.

"I've been better, but I'm looking forward to drinking with you tonight."

"How's Joy?"

"I wish I knew. One minute, she's stable. The next, she's a wreck."

"I remember when your brother died, your mom…" She trails off, waving her hand to a waiter, and orders us both drinks.

"He'll have whiskey, and I'll have vodka cranberry. Make it two of each, please."

I arch an eyebrow, intrigued.

"I'm efficient, Xavier. I'm a mother now." She smiles at me.

"How's Hazel holding up?" I ask.

"If you're asking if she's going to melt down like I did, she will. If you're asking if it'll change her like it did me, no, I don't think it will. She's a different girl than I was back then. She has us and all her friends, and as much as she hates to admit it, she has Hayes."

"Yes, I saw them the other day. Are they still pretending that they don't love each other?"

"It's him, not her. I don't think she's ever denied her feelings for him. And Jett, that was a surprise."

"It was!"

"I always just assumed he and Kadin would've ended up together."

"I don't disagree with you," I answer. "I don't think they would've ended up together without the pregnancy and all this."

"They're doing the right thing, Xavier."

The waiter brings our drinks, and I immediately drain my

first drink. Harper's eyes become huge saucers as she watches me empty my glass.

"That's why you ordered two, right?"

"Umm, no, that's actually not why I ordered two, but we're here, so let's do this." Harper looks to our waiter and says, "We'll take two more of each."

He leaves our table again to put our second order in.

"So, what's next?" Harper asks, playing with the small cocktail straw in her drink.

"The wedding is this weekend, and I guess Jett will be moving in with us." My tone isn't hiding any of my frustration.

"Why are you upset?"

"The last thing I want is to share the limited time I have left with my daughter with a guy." I take a deliberate *sip* of drink, mindful of the reality of not being in my twenties anymore and that my body doesn't recover like it used to.

"Harper, I'm really struggling. Joy's shut down; she won't talk to me about anything beyond household chores and the twins. She's living in denial. Our sex life is nonexistent."

Harper visibly winces, but I continue, "And I feel like I'm tiptoeing around all the time."

"I'm sorry, cuz. What can I do?" she asks, rubbing my arm.

"Let me move in," I say with a half-smile.

She chuckles. "That's not going to get you more time with Olivia."

I shrug with a grin. "Okay, let Jett move in."

She laughs, rolling her eyes as she sits up straighter. "Then I'll have to deal with Hayes more than I already do."

"Well, then, I guess Olivia and I will have to move in."

"You got it! Olivia can sleep with Hazel, and you can take the guest room. It'll be like before when we were younger."

"Except, I won't be sleeping on your couch, and your

husband and our daughters will live there as well."

"Details…details," she says.

Harper finishes off her cocktail then asks, "Are you excited about the baby?"

I run my hand through my hair. "Honestly?"

"Always!"

I exhale sharply and lean forward, resting my elbows on the table. "No."

"No," she repeats, her eyes wide with disbelief.

"No, Harper. My daughter is twenty-two, almost married, and refusing cancer treatment because she's pregnant. No, I'm not excited." I clench my jaw, trying to keep my composure.

Harper tilts her head, studying me. She leans forward, her voice soft. "Can I give you advice?"

I sit back and give her a look. "Why do you even ask? We all know you're going to give it to me."

She chuckles at that, but reaches for the cocktail napkin and fidgets with it. "Don't tell anyone other than me you're not excited about this baby."

I nod. "Obviously, Harper."

"I just don't want you to go to battle with Olivia or Joy over something that's not going to change."

"I know, trust me, I know. Like I said, I just keep my head down when I pass them in the hallway."

"Maybe you should take Olivia out for dinner…*alone.*"

"Maybe," I agree.

"How did we get here?" Harper asks, leaning closer to me. She slurs her words more and more with every sip of her fuchsia drink.

"You took sleeping pills one day, and Gabe found you," I say, my voice carrying the weight of memories. "Which led me to Joy," I say waggling my eyebrows. "Then, before we knew it, you were pregnant with Hazel, so naturally, Joy and I had to hurry up and have a baby too, just so we could raise them together."

Harper grins, shaking her head at the memory.

"And then," I continue, "Hazel and Olivia had to follow Kadin, Hayes and Jett to college, leaving us behind. Somehow, while they were off in Texas, Olivia's whole world turned upside down. And here we are"—I wave my hand around the bar—"just the two of us, alone in a bar getting drunk."

● ● ●

"Last call," the bartender yells.

"Shit, have we been here all night?" I ask, running my hand through my hair as I glance around the dimly lit bar.

"Yeah, and I'm drunk," Harper admits. "You didn't drive, did you?"

"Yes, but I can't drive now," I mutter leaning back in my chair.

"I'll call Gabe to pick us up." Haper fumbles with her clutch, pulling out her phone. She squints at the screen, holding it farther from her face as she tries to focus. After a few seconds, she taps the screen, brings up her favorites list, and presses Gabe's name carefully.

"I'm putting it on speaker so you can hear too." Harper giggles, and I can't help to shake my head. Almost twenty-five years later, Harper is still wreaking havoc on that poor guy.

"Harper, it's 2 a.m. Tell me you and Xavier aren't in jail like the girls were." Gabe answers, his voice groggy but amused

"Hey, babe," Harper says in her best innocent voice. "No, we're not in jail, but I do need you to pick us up." She giggles into the phone.

"There's a thing called Uber for nights that end like this."

"Babe, I'll get kidnapped if I take an Uber home like this," she argues.

"They'll return you, Harper. I swear, if you ever want to know where your daughter gets her bad habits and terrible decision-making, just look in the mirror."

Harper holds the phone out to make sure I can hear him lecture her, which causes us to laugh so loud that the table next to us is trying to listen.

"So, you'll get us?"

"Sorry, man, I tried to tell her not to overindulge," I shout into her phone even though it's not needed.

"Gabe," she slurs. "He's lying; he just kept ordering us drinks."

"Send me your location. I'll be there in a few." Gabe's voice comes through, calm but resigned.

"I love you, Gabe," she slurs again into the phone, blowing a dramatic kiss.

"I love you, Gabe," I playfully mimic her, putting my arm around her shoulder as we collapse into a fit of drunken laughter, loud enough that people at the nearby table glance over at us again, amused by the spectacle.

# Chapter 28

## OLIVIA

"Today is the day," my mom whispers from the doorway of my bedroom.

"Good morning, Mom."

"Are you hungry? I'm making waffles for your brothers and eggs for your dad."

"No, I'm good. I'll have an apple when I get up to take my pills."

"Okay, I'll see you in the kitchen in a few," she says as she slowly closes my door, allowing me a minute to wake up.

Today is supposed to be the happiest day of my life, but it's not. I think the happiest day of my life was when I was eight and our family took a vacation to Hawaii. Kadin's and Hazel's family went as well. It was an all-inclusive resort that provided childcare for all of us kids. My mom was so carefree, not a care in the world. She and my dad were so happy. Us girls ran around from dusk to dawn, which is shocking since my Aunt Harper usually never let us out of her sight. I think Hazel and my Uncle Gabe had a silent agreement that if he kept her drunk all week, Hazel would keep her room clean the entire school year. He kept his end of the bargain, so Kadin and I helped Hazel keep hers. Every weekend, we would spend two hours hanging clothes and cleaning. Have I ever mentioned my cousin is a slob? I feel sorry for her future husband. Speaking of the future husband. I grab my phone while I have a second to myself and text her and Kadin.

*Me* – So, while I'm not vomiting or getting married, can you tell me what's going on with Hayes? And don't lie to me.

*Hazel* – Good morning to you, too. Why are we talking about Hayes on your wedding day?

*Me* – Why not?

*Hazel* – Because today is supposed to be about you, not me.

*Me* – Today, tomorrow, and the next will be about me. Come on, give me something here. My life is all baby and death all the time. Give me something good.

*Hazel* – You know you're dark, right?

*Me* – I've always been dark.

*Hazel* – Not like this. This is some next-level shit.

*Kadin* – OMG, it's too early. Why are you guys blowing up my phone?

*Me* – Kadin, what's going on with Hayes and Hazel?

Kadin has left the conversation.

*Me* – What, you are serious? HAZEL, what is happening?

*Hazel* – Nothing; he said he loves me and proposed, and I told him that I couldn't deal with him right now.

Olivia left the conversation.

Immediately, I FaceTime Hazel. Her sleepy face pops up on my phone, head resting against a pillow, her light brown hair disheveled. She's clearly still in bed just like me. "I can't believe you didn't tell me. Why?" I ask, my voice surprisingly hoarse for being awake for more than a few minutes.

Hazel props herself up slightly, her eyes squinting as she tries to focus on the screen. "Are you in bed still?"

I shift, pulling the covers up higher, and glance around at my own tangled sheets. "Yes, why?"

She gives me a small laugh. "What, did you just wake up thinking about Hayes and me and decide today *on your wedding day* was the day you were going to interrogate me about it?"

"Basically. What's wrong with that? Instead of rushing to the bathroom to throw up, I figured I'd be a normal twenty-two-year-old and text my cousin to see how her life was going."

"My life is great. My cousin is getting married today, her baby is healthy, and the guy that I've wanted to marry since

I was in fifth grade proposed and promised to wait for me when I told him I wasn't ready. So, to answer your question, I'm great. How are you feeling?"

"I told you I feel okay today."

"That's not what I asked, Olivia. How are you feeling?" she said, drawing out the 'e' sound.

"I'm okay," I insist.

"Olivia, you know we're on FaceTime, and I can see your face, right? Your mouth is saying one thing, but your expression is saying the opposite."

"I'm…" My voice trails off as I try to find the right words to describe my precise feelings. "I'm fine, but to say this is my ideal day would be a lie."

Hazel just nods, so I continue.

"Marrying Jett isn't a bad thing; forcing Jett to marry me because I'm pregnant and dying is really unfair."

"Umm, I hardly think you're forcing Jett to marry you, Olivia."

"Aren't I, though? If I weren't dying, we wouldn't be getting married. He'd be back at school talking to an agent, preparing to be scouted, but instead, he's getting tied down to a dying, pregnant girl."

"Olivia, first, Jett is a grown man. He chose this path; you didn't force him into anything. Second, football is done; he's proven himself. Jett left everything on the field during the playoffs; either he's getting picked up by a team, or he's not. That has nothing to do with you. Your parents and his parents are stepping up for May if… Well, you know…if they need to help. Stop blaming yourself for getting pregnant; it takes two to tango."

"No, Hazel, you don't get it. I'm dying. In a year or two, I'll be gone, and Jett will be left alone to care for our baby.

It's not fair!"

"Olivia. Admit you're not ready to die. You don't need to hide behind the pregnancy. You're twenty-two years old. People have babies at our age. They don't die."

"I feel like my death is going to shatter everyone."

"It will, Olivia. You're going to shatter everyone's heart, and nothing will ever be the same. When I walk down the aisle someday, it'll break me that my cousin can't be my maid of honor. And, when I have a daughter, there will be a gaping hole where our girls shared memories should've been. But, and this is crucial, Olivia – it's not your choice. This ending wasn't written by you. So, please stop blaming yourself?"

"My dad's not happy about the wedding," I add, completely side-stepping the weight of her words.

"No one will ever be good enough for you, Olivia, so I can't promise that if this wedding was in five years, with no pregnancy or illness, your dad wouldn't be happy, so don't dwell on that."

•  •  •

My dad and I stand staring at two huge mahogany church doors. All I can think about is how beautiful the woodwork is.

"How long do you think it took someone to engrave these?" I ask, looking up at my dad.

He's wearing an all-black tuxedo at my request. My mom loves black, and since I won't get to see everyone at my funeral, I asked that everyone attending wear black except for me, *of course*, and my bridesmaids, Hazel and Kadin. Both of them are wearing emerald green.

"Really, Olivia? We're about to walk down your wedding aisle, and you're asking me about the engraving on the doors?"

"I think they're pretty," I reply with a shrug. "Dad, they can't start without us, and someone put a lot of effort into the doors only to be noticed, so I'm noticing them."

He chuckles and says, "They're nice doors, Olivia. But are we standing here admiring doors or taking a minute to ourselves? I'm okay with either option. I'd just like to know what we're doing here when we should be through there." My dad points to where we're standing then the doors.

"We're admiring the door while stalling here alone, taking a minute to ourselves when we should be down there," I answer him.

With a kiss to the top of my head, he quietly reassures me, "We can stand back here as long as you want and admire these doors; just let me know when you're ready to get married."

# Chapter 29

## KADIN

Her dress, with its low-cut front, showcases a satin bodice and an elegantly backless design. The empire waist allows Baby May to make her presence known as Olivia and her dad float down the aisle. I glance at Jett, but his eyes are fixed on Olivia, seemingly oblivious to the fifty people filling the small church around us. Hazel squeezes my hand, pulling my attention from Jett back to the reason we're here.

Olivia's dad places her hand into Jett's, and the pastor begins the ceremony. Most of what he says becomes white noise as I watch Jett and Olivia standing hand in hand, wondering what today would have been like if things had been different. Would Jett and Olivia still be getting married? I had always assumed it would be Hayes, Hazel, and maybe Jett and I. But circumstances are what they are, and Olivia looks radiant.

The pastor says, "And you may kiss the bride."

The church erupts into cheers, returning my attention to Jett and Olivia just in time for their first kiss as a married couple. They're perfect together. I want to keep this memory of Olivia forever.

Jett and Olivia take a limousine to Hazel's house for the reception. In the backyard, there are several round tables, each with eight chairs and a place card. Huge white flower arrangements adorn the middle of each table, making it hard to see the head table. The decorations are emerald green, complementing Hazel and my bridesmaids' dresses.

The DJ is playing soft eighties music in the corner, filling the air with gentle, nostalgic notes. The melodies create a warm, intimate atmosphere, perfectly complementing the soft glow of the string lights hanging above. Guests mingle, their laughter and quiet conversations blending harmoniously with the music.

I look around and see Olivia and Jett already on the dance floor, swaying slowly to the rhythm, lost in their own world. Her head rests on his shoulder, eyes closed. Nearby, Hayes and Hazel share a quiet moment, their usual banter replaced with soft murmurs as they lean in close, whispering to each other.

My heart swells with a mix of joy and melancholy as I watch the people I care about find moments of happiness amid the chaos of our lives. What will my future look like? Will I go overseas and play soccer professionally? Hayes and Hazel will most certainly be married by this time next year, Jett and Olivia are already married.

If I do go overseas, I will most definitely be alone, thousands of miles from my friends and family. They'll all be here, together, connected by May, sharing in each other's lives while I drift further away.

As they build their lives together, I can't help but feel like a spectator, watching from the sidelines, forever on the outside looking in.

As the song changes to another eighties classic, I feel a hand on my shoulder. Turning, I see Jett's warm smile as he extends his hand to me.

"Care for a dance?" he asks, his eyes twinkling with the same familiar mischief.

I glance around the dance floor to see Olivia swaying with Jensen, one of her twin brothers, so I smile back, taking his hand. "I'd love to," I reply, letting him lead me to the dance floor.

Hazel and Hayes have their arms out, waiting to welcome me into their dance circle. As the four of us sway to the music, surrounded by love, I realize that despite everything, I'll be okay, our group will be okay. And maybe, despite all my worries, I'll never be alone for too long.

As the night progresses and the soft eighties' tunes transition into late nineties' dance music, Hazel and I find ourselves on the dance floor more often than at our assigned table. Hazel has pulled her dad out there at least three times, and, of course, I've had my father out there, too. She's even managed to get all the moms up, teaching them how to 'dougie'. Hazel and her antics have the photographer working overtime—and she actually ends up teaching him a dance or two.

And that's Hazel. Despite the circumstances of the day, she manages to make everything fun. Her infectious energy and spontaneous spirit light up the room, reminding everyone that even in the midst of chaos, joy can always find a way.

## Chapter 30

OLIVIA

"Mom!" I shout from the hallway.

"I'll be right down; I'm writing in my journal," she calls from upstairs.

I take a deep breath and try to stay calm, but the urgency in my voice breaks through, "It's May, my water broke. I need to go to the hospital."

There's a pause, and then I hear hurried footsteps as my mom sprints down the stairs, her face pales as she takes me in. "What? You're not due for a few weeks; it's too early!"

"Tell her that," I say, pointing at my belly. "Because I'm pretty sure I didn't just pee myself, which can only mean she's coming, ready or not!"

On cue, sheer chaos erupts as my mom rushes back upstairs. There's intelligible yelling as she looks for her shoes and tries to put them on all while trying to get my dad out of the restroom. My mom, generally graceful, is everything but that right now. By the sounds coming from upstairs, she is falling all over herself, trying to get back down the stairs to me.

"Mom, calm down. We have time," I try to reassure her,

rubbing my belly and moving slightly out of the way so she doesn't barrel me over on her way back down.

"Where's your dad?" she asks, looking around as if he's hiding from her.

"Upstairs where you left him," I say, shrugging my shoulders.

"Xavier!" she screams.

I wince. "Mom, calm down. You literally just made the baby kick."

She ignores me. "Boys!" she screams again, but this time, it's aimed at Nolen and Jensen.

This time, May is prepared, and I can picture her with her little baby's hands covering her ears.

"Yeah, Mom," the boys casually holler in unison from upstairs.

"Your sister is having the baby. We have to go!"

"Can we just come when it's done?" Jensen yells back down.

She looks at me, eyebrows raised, seeking my approval. I nod, giving my unspoken permission. The boys could care less about waiting hours at the hospital. They're seniors this year, and babies don't make the list of their priorities. Football, video games, girls, and, oddly enough, each other, but I guess that's part of being a twin.

My dad jogs down the stairs, grabbing my overnight bag as he passes. He glances between my mom and me and quips, "Shall we stand here all day, or are we going to have a baby today?"

"Where's Jett?" my mom asks.

"He's with Hayes, and they're already on their way to the hospital with Hazel. Hazel has already told her parents and Aunt Roxy. So, if we wait around any longer, we could possibly be the last people there," I say, trying to get a move on.

"Well, there's no baby without you, so at least we're in the right place," my dad says in a futile attempt at one of his famous dad jokes.

"Dad, unless you want to deliver this baby, we better get a move on," I say; just as a contraction hits me like a cement truck. "*Oh my god!*" I scream. "I can't do this," I say, holding my stomach folded at the waist. "I'm going to die." Oddly enough, it is not a lie, but these two find zero humor in my twisted thoughts, so I decide to keep that to myself.

I grab my dad by the arm, still hunched over. "Dad, I can't do this. I need drugs. Make this stop. I can't take it."

Rubbing my back, he says, "Olivia, it'll pass. Let's count to ten, and it'll be gone."

In unison, we count, "One, two, three…"

"It's gone," I say, standing straight now.

"We have to go, Xavier. Help her to the car," my mom says, her voice tight with barely hidden panic.

· · ·

We arrive at the hospital in record time, pulling up to the emergency entrance. The bright red sign glows above us, casting an eerie glow on the pavement. Jett, Hazel and Hayes are pacing anxiously near the entrance. As we pull to a stop, I roll down my window just in time to catch Jett's voice, loud and frustrated.

"What the hell took so long?" Jett shouts, his voice echoing in the parking lot.

I narrow my eyes and raise an eyebrow, giving him the slightest tilt of my head, forcing him to immediately backtrack.

"What I meant was," he quickly recovers, running a hand over his face, "Hi, how are you feeling? Are we all ready to have a baby today?"

"Let's go, people. Lady with a baby!" Hazel shouts, waving her arms for anyone to pay attention to her.

My dad chuckles, shaking his head as he comes around to help me out of the car. "Hazel, you know you're exactly like your mother, right?"

She gives him an exaggerated wink while she points both index fingers at him.

My mom bursts out with a wheelchair, and my dad sets me gingerly on it. Hazel comes around, shoves herself between my dad and the handles, and shouts, with one finger pointed to the sky, "I'll drive. Everyone, follow me!"

My parents are going to kill her before this day is over. Hazel rushes me through the front door, yelling, "Lady with a baby, we need a doctor! My cousin is having a baby! Move aside, lady with a baby." She leans down to my ear and whispers, laughing, "I've always wanted to do that."

"You're going to get us kicked out," I hiss.

"Olivia, don't be a stick in the mud," she says, dismissing me.

"Hazel, you know I'm about to push a human out of my vagina, right?"

"Wait, I thought you had to have a c-section?"

"It's too late; my water broke," I trail off, glancing around, trying to find some sort of reassurance. My hands fidget. "I mean, I think it's too late," I add, my voice wavering slightly as I search for certainty I clearly don't have. I feel panic rising. "I don't know, but if my doctor will let me, I'm pushing her out."

"*Ouch*!" I yell as another contraction hits, my hands gripping the handles.

"What's happening?" Hazel asks, abruptly stopping as she pushes me in the wheelchair. "She was fine a second ago."

Instantly, I'm surrounded by several nurses, and they're wheeling me up to the maternity floor, my mom right by my side. I yell over my shoulder and hold up my hand for Jett. "Are you coming?"

"I'm right behind you, babe," he says as he hits Hayes in the arm. "I'm going to be a dad today."

"I'm right behind you guys too, Olivia," Hazel shouts.

"You're coming in, right?" I ask her as they load me into the elevator.

A smile overtakes her lips just before the elevator door closes. "I wouldn't miss this for the world, cuz."

• • •

"She looks like Olivia!" Hazel says, eyes wide with amazement as she stands over May. She's just staring at her mesmerized, while May rests peacefully in the bassinet they placed her in right after she was born.

"She looks like me," Jett argues. "You've never seen baby pictures of me, and that's exactly what I looked like as a baby."

"Jett, you've never been as pretty as this baby right here." Hazel teases, a playful smirk spreading across her face.

The nurse places our baby girl on my chest, and Jett comes over to kiss her forehead and then repeats the gesture on me.

"She's perfection," he says.

And she is; her skin is pale, with red splotches everywhere. Her blue eyes peer up at me, and she has orange hair, which I'm secretly hoping turns blonde.

"Jett, can you please go tell everyone to come in and meet May."

Hazel sits next to me on the bed. "You did good, Mom." A tear escapes her eyes, and I rest my head against her arm.

"Just because she's here doesn't mean I'm dying, Hazel."

"I know, it's just one more thing off our checklist. I feel like soon there will be only one more thing left."

"Yeah." I sigh as one of my tears hits May on the forehead.

In typical fashion, Hazel breaks the sadness by saying, "Stop drowning my niece with your tears already."

There's a soft knock on the door, and instantly, my room is flooded with people. Jett's mom, my mom, my dad, my Aunt Harper, and Aunt Roxy are all crowded around May and me; their expressions are pure bliss. I lift my gaze. Hazel is tucked under Dad's arm. Her attempts to discreetly wipe away tears do not go unnoticed by me.

Despite her usual bubbly personality and optimistic demeanor, I see the hidden layers of sorrow and fear beneath the surface. It's as if they're fighting to break free from the façade she wears so bravely, and in that moment, I can't help but feel the weight of her unspoken emotions.

# Chapter 31

## HAZEL

Today is May's first birthday, and it has to be perfect, not for me or even for May but for Olivia. If things don't start to improve, this could be her only opportunity to celebrate a birthday with her daughter. Kadin and I have been running all over town, functioning solely on caffeine and donuts. We split up an hour ago to try to cover more ground. I'm currently sitting at The Grind waiting for her to get here so we can refuel with coffee and a sandwich.

Olivia hasn't been feeling great lately; in fact, I don't think she's felt well for the last year and a half. The cancer is taking a devastating toll on her body. She has lost twenty pounds she couldn't afford to lose since giving birth to May, and her headaches keep her bedridden most days. Some days, she's so confused that she couldn't find her left hand if it weren't attached to her body.

I watch her struggle, my heart aching with every wince of pain and every moment of confusion, and I can't help but wonder if things would have been different if she had agreed to treatment after May was born, as she promised. But she never did, and now we're left with the harsh reality of her choices.

Seeing Olivia like this, a shadow of her vibrant self is one of the hardest things I've ever experienced. She's fighting so hard, but the battle is relentless, and it's taking everything from her.

The stress of our impending future is taking a toll on me, but I remind myself that my battle of emotions is nothing compared to her physical battle. I'm going to push all fears deep down in the pits of my being, only to let them resurface the next time Olivia gets sick.

Jett will be home today for the party, and we're all excited to see him. He was drafted by the Mustangs, San Diego's professional football team, so he's been spending the majority of his time down there. This means Kadin and I have pretty much been living at Olivia's house with her and May.

Olivia spent the last week in the hospital but was released yesterday, just in time for the party and the twins' high-school graduation.

My Aunt Joy kept May while Kadin and I stayed with Olivia in the hospital. She brings May every day to see Olivia, but I know it's hard on Olivia when she leaves every night to go home with someone else. Hayes is *always* around to help, and in another life, that would be something of a girl's dream, but I need alone time with Olivia. I have forever to be with Hayes.

Jett checks in every night on both May and Olivia over FaceTime. I know he feels guilty for being away, but Olivia is very realistic when it comes to where they stand. He needs to play football before he can't anymore. A football career comes and goes quicker than a good pair of running shoes. One injury and it's all over. Just look at Hayes; he's a perfect example of how quickly it can be over. One bad hit to the shoulder and your entire childhood dream is a distant memory of what was.

I'm hopeful she'll feel good enough to attend a few games

since his home stadium is in California, and she won't have to fly anywhere. We can all road trip down there like old times when we'd drive all over to watch Hayes play in high school. Maybe it'll make us all feel like kids again.

Don't get me wrong—we aren't kids—but I also feel like we were forced into an alternate universe that forced up to grow up really fast the last year and a half. One minute, we were in Texas partying every weekend, and Olivia and Jett were on and off, on and off. Then, she's pregnant and has cancer and we're dropping out of school to move home, before she's getting married and having a kid.

And I'm here trying to hold onto every memory I can While also trying to forget them. It's becoming increasingly hard for my brain to separate what's supposed to be stored forever and what's supposed to be erased. My mom always used to say, *"Good memories embed themselves in your heart, but bad ones get embedded in your head and live there forever. Your heart fails you at every turn, and your head never forgets, never forgives."* I never really understood what she meant by that, but as the days pass and Olivia's illness progresses, I'm unfortunately growing all too familiar with the meaning behind it.

"Hey. Did you order for us?" Kadin says, coming up behind me, snapping me out of my thoughts.

I stutter, "Uh… No…not yet."

"What's wrong?" she says as she throws a bunch of bags on the empty chair next to me at our table.

Shaking my head dismissively I say, "Nothing. You just surprised me."

She cocks her head to one side. "Seriously, are we lying to each other now?"

"No, I…" I trail off again, trying to figure out what to tell her. Do I tell her the truth that I feel like I'm slowly dying inside alongside Olivia? Or do I continue to lie to both of us?

"Hello," she says, waving a hand in front of my face. "Earth to Hazel."

Looking up at her as I sink a little into my chair, I say, "I'm just thinking about life, that's all." I mean, that's technically not lying.

She swirls her hands as she lifts an eyebrow, obviously trying to get more details from me.

"You're seriously as bad as my mom," I say.

"And that's a bad thing; why? Stop lying to me. We don't lie to each other."

"I'm not lying. I'm just upset about Olivia. There, are you happy?" I feel the sting of tears behind my eyes but blink them away.

"No, I'm not happy. Do you think I'm happy you're hurting and silently dying inside? Do you think I'm happy that one of my best friends is withering away right in front of us? Do you think I'm happy that my mom is going to have to pick up the broken pieces of not only my broken heart but Aunt Joy's heart?

"And lastly, and certainly the most selfish, but since we're not lying to each other. Do you think I'm happy to be here and not back at school playing soccer?"

"Kadin, I'm sorry. I don't know what to say." I gently place my hand on hers, giving it a comforting squeeze.

"I hate to complain about how I'm feeling because it feels so insignificant compared to what Olivia is going through."

"You're allowed to be sad, Hazel. You don't have to be strong all the time for everyone."

"I know, it's just hard to complain about being sad when I have my entire life ahead of me and..." I trail off

"Say it! Say it, Hazel! You not saying it isn't going to make it not happen." Kadin isn't one for confrontation, ever.

Until this moment, I didn't even know she knew how to be confrontational. Her olive complexion has a pinkish tone to it, a telltale sign of how upset she is. But now, I'm wondering if she's really upset at me or using me as an outlet for her pain.

"I know that, but me saying I'm sad will not stop it happening either. It's just easier for me to stay busy."

"Live in denial." It's not a question it's a statement.

"Yeah, sure, live in denial," I agree.

"Have you told her about Hayes? Have you told your parents about Hayes?"

"What the fuck." I draw out 'fuck' for effect. "What is your malfunction today, Kadin? Why are you coming at me like this? Yes, Olivia knows we're together. Of course, my parents know we're together. They just don't know the extent of it. And they're not going to find out either because I don't want to deal with my mom." I give her a look of warning.

"Kadin, I love you and don't want to fight with you, but you're testing every cell in my body right now. I'm about to get up and walk out of here, all while telling you to fuck off. I'm sorry you're not happy about being home away from your old teammates. I'm sorry you're not playing soccer.

"I told you not to come home. I told you to stay at school, but you never fucking listen. You just do whatever you think everyone else wants, and then you throw a temper tantrum about it later."

I stand up, grab my purse, and walk out, leaving her there speechless. Kadin and I don't usually argue. Come to think about it, we never argue. Our personalities are so similar that there's never a reason. I'm her biggest fan. Olivia and I are cousins, so arguing with her comes naturally. We argue and make up. We're family. Kadin and I aren't. We make an effort to be best friends, but it's never really been an effort because everything with us is easy.

# Chapter 32

## KADIN

I watch Hazel storm out of the door and drop my head into my hands, screaming into them to muffle the sound. A few nearby customers shot me curious glances, but I barely notice. *Why did I just say all that stuff to Hazel?* I literally started a fight with her for no reason. I'm stressed, yes, but could I just tell her that without attacking her? Yes, the answer to that question is yes. Even worse she would've understood if I was just honest with her. And Hayes, why did I even bring him up?

I feel as if I'm so stressed about something that hasn't happened yet that I've completely stopped living in the present. I'm plagued with regret about leaving school, and the guilt I feel about being upset is overwhelming me now. I didn't take online classes for my diploma, hoping that maybe I could return to school and still play, but I don't even know if that's an option.

• • •

I pause for a minute at the door, listening to the quiet hum of their conversation. The tension from earlier still weighs on me as I knock gently, then push the door open.

"Can I come in?" I ask, peeking my head around the door. Olivia is sitting cross-legged on her bed and looks up with her signature sweet smile.

"Hey..." she draws out the word in her melodic voice.

I'm loud and goofy. Hazel is loud and in charge. There's a presence to her. We call her Camp Director Hazel. She gets it from her mom, but Olivia is soft-spoken and will follow you to the ends of the earth even if she doesn't want to. Remember, she ended up in jail with Hazel and I for no reason. She didn't drink, she didn't fight, she just followed us to jail. That's Olivia.

I glance over at Hazel, who is standing in front of the mirror, curling a strand of her hair. The iron sizzles slightly as it releases a perfect wave. She turns briefly to see who entered the room. The second she sees me, her eyes narrow, and she whips back to Olivia's reflection.

"Oh, no. No, no, no!" Olivia says. "This is not happening today. You are not fighting on my daughter's first birthday. Absolutely not. You two are not ruining today for me."

Hazel's eyes flick to me again with a smug look on her face, which almost sets me off for the second time today, but Olivia is right, I was wrong back at The Grind. I raise my hands in surrender and say, "I'm sorry. I came to apologize to Hazel."

Hazel doesn't say anything as her gaze moves from Olivia's reflection to me now.

"Say something!" I demand.

"I have nothing to say," she retorts, tilting her head with a glare before turning back to the mirror.

"What the hell is going on?" Olivia asks.

"She's a jackass," Hazel blurts.

Trying to stifle a laugh at her choice of insults, I say, "Umm, that's not called for. Is it?"

"Isn't it?" Hazel fires back, sounding like a five-year-old child now.

"Can someone just tell me what's going on?" Olivia pleads.

"Something is wrong with Kadin, and she's starting fights with me, so I'm giving her what she wants…a fight."

"Oh no, you're not!" Olivia insists. "You're going to make me pull the 'I'm dying' card, aren't you?" She glances between us, her voice half-serious, half-playful as she tries to defuse the situation.

"No!" I interrupt her before she can lecture us about how she's dying as if we don't know, and that's what caused this whole argument in the first place. "I'm sorry," I say, looking at Hazel. "I was a *jackass*," I say, using air quotes to drive home her choice of words.

"I accept your apology," she says, looking away again with a smug look on her face.

I roll my eyes and continue, "Hazel, I'm sorry, I really am. I was out of line, and I'm just having a hard time." I look down to the floor and tap the floor with the toe of my Chucks. "It's hard to be home with all the kids. I don't have an outlet like I did when I played soccer. It's a lot, and I know I'm not allowed to feel like this because you," I say, pointing at Olivia, "obviously, have it worse than any of us."

"Hold on," Olivia interjects, her voice firm as she raises a hand to both of us. "Are you both pretending that my impending death isn't affecting you? Do you feel like you're not allowed to be in pain because I'm dying and you're not? So, I'm the only one allowed to grieve what I gave up or will be missing out on?"

Her words hit hard, and she continues with a mix of

frustration and sorrow, "Even worse than that thought process is that you two honestly think that anyone around you believes your happy-go-lucky façade? Hazel, you're keeping yourself so busy with God knows what to avoid reality, which includes admitting you and Hayes are together. And, Kadin, you barely come out of your room, you don't work out anymore, you avoid us. I don't know how to make this any clearer to you both. I'm dying, and you are not. So, please do us a favor and stop acting like you are."

"You're right," I say, shrugging because she is. There is nothing I can say to dispute her argument.

"You're right," Hazel agrees.

"I know I'm right. I'm always right," Olivia says, flipping her freshly curled hair over her shoulder with a playful smirk.

We all burst into laughter, the tension easing between us, just as there's a knock on Olivia's door.

"Come in!" she hollers.

"How's my girl?" Jett barges in full of excitement and wraps his arms around Olivia from behind her. He looks at her in the mirror. "You look beautiful," he says, kissing her on the cheek.

He looks over to Hazel and I, his expression lifting as he points toward the door with a playful grin.

"What?" Hazel asks, throwing her hands up in mock confusion.

"Out!" Jett teases, waving his hand toward the door. "Go make yourself busy setting up so I can spend some time with my wife without you two gawking at us."

"Eww," Hazel scrunches her nose, making a face, before grabbing my arm and pulling me out of the bedroom.

As the door closes, Hazel spins me around to face her. "Are you ready for today?" Without giving me time to respond, she continues, "May's first birthday... It feels like she was born yesterday." Again, without waiting for a reply, she turns to head downstairs, where the party is already coming together, thanks to our moms.

My Aunt Joy is holding May—her short, brown hair and blue eyes remind me so much of Olivia's. May is a carbon copy of her mother. She has Olivia's fairness, complete with a sprinkling of freckles across her cheeks. I can't help but smile at how much she's grown. I can't help but wish she never changes.

The living room is filled with pastel-pink-colored balloons (we're determined to make her fall in love with pink), and a large '1' made of flowers stands proudly in the center. The smell of fresh-baked cupcakes fills the air, making my stomach growl.

In the backyard, there's a picnic area set up with a pastel-pink blanket for May to sit on with her cake. Friends and family have already started gathering, their laughter filling the air.

A while later, Jett and Olivia emerge from inside the house, and Olivia lifts May from Aunt Joy's arms, kissing her baby softly on the cheek. They mingle with guests for a bit before Hazel announces with a playful smile, holding up her phone, "Alright, everyone, it's time for May to smash her cake."

# Chapter 33

## HAZEL

I run downstairs and yell, *"Come in!"*

"You ready?" Hayes asks, looking me up and down as I reach the last threshold of our staircase.

I raise an eyebrow, playfully swatting at his arm. "Don't look at me like that in my parents' house," I whisper.

"Like what?" he asks, pulling me into a hug, his breath is warm against my ear. His tone is innocent, but the guilty gleam in eyes says otherwise.

"Like you want to devour me," I murmur, my pulse quickening as his arms tighten around me.

"Please tell me you don't have Jett's number and name on the back of that jersey, Hazel. We talked about this in college. No guy's girl should wear any other man's name on her body."

I scoff at him as I turn around and point over my shoulders with my thumbs. "No name, no number. Listen, this is an archaic and wellll"—I draw out the word for effect—"stupid rule. But, in solidarity with my ex-football-playing boyfriend's feelings, I'm wearing a blank jersey."

"Boyfriend," he teases me.

"Shut up, dummy," I say nudging him.

"When are you going to marry me, Hazel?" he asks, leaning close to my ear.

"Hi, Hayes," my mom says as she makes her way down the stairs, saving me from having to have this conversation with Hayes again. Will we get married? Of course, we will. I've wanted to marry him since we were kids but now is not the time. He finished college online and received his degree. Currently, he's coaching high-school football at our alma mater and has also opened a strength and training facility for kids near his house. Jett's presence on opening day was a huge draw for the community and helped max out membership. He has also agreed to host a few summer camps for kids when they're out of school.

"Hey, Mrs. Jones." Hayes cheerfully lifts a hand to my mom, and I roll my eyes at the two of them.

"Where's Dad?" I ask.

"He's coming. Are you guys riding with us to the game or just caravanning down?"

Hayes looks at me, and I immediately answer. "I told you we're staying down there tonight, so we're going to drive. Olivia and Kadin are driving down with us."

"Hmmm." She looks between the two of us, then continues, "Shame, I was hoping the two of you would spend the night down there alone."

"Ewww. Mom! Stop!"

"Stop what?" My dad asks, walking downstairs.

"You're wife, that's what."

"I don't want to know then," he says, covering his ears. "We have to go." He continues, "We're driving Joy, Xavier, Roxanne, and Chris."

"How are you all going to fit?" I ask.

"I rented a van." My dad is so proud right now, and I burst out laughing—real loud, genuine laughter.

"You rented a van?" I say between laughter.

"Yeah, it's one of those big luxury vans." He looks between my mom and me and asks, "What's so funny? Seriously, did I miss something?"

"You're an old man, Dad. You sound like a grandpa."

"Well, unless you two have something to tell me." He glares at Hayes. "I'm not…right? Hayes…"

"No, sir, you're not a grandpa. Or…you're not going…" He is stammering all over his words and can't put a sentence together if his life depends on it right now.

Hayes puts his hands in his pocket, surrendering. My dad puts his hand on Hayes's shoulder and says, "I'm just kidding, son, but if you think you want to marry my daughter, you better get some thicker skin or these two," he says, gesturing between my mom and me, "will eat you alive. A piece of advice…"

Hayes nods, but my dad never asked for permission; it is a suggestion. "Don't you dare propose to my daughter without asking me."

My mom shakes her head in disapproval, and I know my dad is in so much trouble. So, in my second attempt at solidarity today, I hold up my hand and high-five my dad just as I turn to walk out of the door, dragging a very shocked and terrified Hayes Emerson behind me as I whisper so only he can hear.

"Should we tell him now or wait to tell him you already proposed to me on the side of the road without a ring?"

• • •

The stadium buzzes with anticipation. Me and my parents are sporting red and black, the Mustangs' colors. May has red noise-canceling headphones covering both of her cute little ears and a jersey sporting her last name on the back. She's sitting in the middle of everyone, being passed around more than the football currently in play on the field in front of us. Her face is blue from endless amounts of cotton candy.

Hayes looks at me and puts his hand on my knee, pulling me from my thoughts. "You should try to create good memories today instead of dwelling on things you can't control."

I place my hand on top of his, and it's impossible to miss the grin on Kadin's face as she watches from my opposite side. I throw a piece of popcorn at her, and it sticks to her hair. May doesn't miss what just happened and escapes the grasp of her mom's arms and crawls across leg after leg to get to me.

"Do not give her popcorn, Hazel," my mom yells at me as she leans forward with at least three other individuals between us. I pretend not to hear her as I put my hand over my ears. How does she even see what's happening here? For someone who thought she could not keep another human alive, she is pretty keen on everything happening around her. So, being typical me, I hold a piece of popcorn up to May's lips and say, "No biting, just lick the butter and salt off." Then, I proceeded to demonstrate what she's allowed to do. I catch my mom out of the corner of my eye, shaking her head at my defiance and I give her a little wave with a big fake smile strung across my face.

The Mustangs' theme song fills the entire stadium, eliciting cheers as everyone rises to watch their favorite team burst through the tunnel, engulfed in thick, white smoke. Amidst the excitement, I stand with May in my arms, swaying to the music as she clings to my shoulders, her smile radiant. Jett emerges from the smoke; the crowd erupts into cheers, and

May Shouts, "Daddy!" with delight as I point out Jett sprinting toward the home bench.

"There's your daddy. Say hi, Daddy," I exclaim.

May echoes, "Daddy, Daddy."

Jett, now helmet-free, rushes closer to our seats, his pride palpable. He shares a loving glance with Olivia before blowing a kiss to May, which she pretends to eat. I guide her to kiss her hand and throw kisses back to her daddy.

Olivia captures the scene on her cell phone, preserving the family moment for eternity, and a pang of guilt strikes me to my core. Olivia should be in this video with May, not me. How many opportunities like this will she have to share with her daughter?

"Hey!" she shouts at me, grabbing not only my attention but everyone's around us.

I look over at her, and she shakes her head at me, knowing exactly where my mind just wandered. Everyone is looking at us, engaged in our silent exchange. I nod at her in understanding and kiss May on the forehead as Hayes wraps his hand around my waist to pull me into him.

The game ends in a victory for the Mustangs. We all wait for Jett outside the player's room. All the parents get their hugs in and leave for the long drive home shortly after their goodbyes. Kadin, Jett, Olivia, Hayes, and I are staying down here tonight with May. It's just like old times when we were back at school, except we don't get drunk, and we have a baby now.

*Chapter 34*

HAZEL

My Aunt Joy answers the door in her black joggers and oversized hoodie, her eyes have dark circles visible beneath them. She moves slowly, as if each step weighs her down. Her posture is slouched. It's as though she's been harboring a secret from the world, perhaps afraid that acknowledging Olivia's illness will make it all too real. She seems reluctant to speak it into existence, as if by not speaking of it, Olivia won't succumb to the reality of her disease, which is why today is too important to put off.

Olivia has lost ten additional pounds in the past three months. Her face is gaunt and even paler than usual. Her fair skin resembles buttermilk, sprinkled with freckles across the bridge of her nose, reminiscent of her mom's. Her normally rosy cheeks lately lack their usual lively color. Her champagne-colored hair has thinned, not due to treatment but because of medication and malnutrition. Meals are a struggle, often not staying down for long.

"Hazel, what are you doing here?" My aunt's clearly surprised to see me but still steps aside to allow me entrance.

"Didn't Olivia tell you we're having a girl's day?"

"A girl's day?" she repeats.

"Yeah, we're going to get mani pedis with shoulder massages and walk around the mall, then maybe go see a movie."

"Where's Kadin?"

"On her way," I holler as I make my way to Olivia's room.

I don't bother knocking before I enter because, well…why would I? I peer in as I slowly enter. "Hey, whatcha doing?" I ask.

She looks up quickly, eyes wide, her breath catching for a minute. "You scared me" she says, pressing a hang to her chest. "I'm trying to write"

"Writing what?" I ask because she's obviously not going to make this easy.

"Sit down. I need to talk to you."

I take a deep breath as I throw myself onto her bed. When Olivia says, '*I need to talk to you*' it's never good. "What's wrong?"

"Nothing is wrong."

"Then why am I sitting down for this?"

She chuckles as she says, "Because I don't want you standing over me, and I need to sit down."

I don't really believe her, but I'm going with the easy-breezy vibe she's giving off. She gets up from her desk, walks over to the closet, and pulls out a clear storage container. It's not too big but larger than a shoe box, and it doesn't fit on my lap.

"What's this?" I ask, looking up at her. I put my hands on both sides and balance it on my legs.

"It's for May."

"And…" I say, drawing out the 'a' for effect. "Help me out here, Olivia. You know I'm not good at this." By 'this', I mean the guessing game of '*what's on my mind today*'.

Olivia sits next to me, her movements slow and methodical.

"Are you feeling okay?" I ask.

"I don't ever feel okay anymore, Hazel, but I'm alive." The inflection in her voice makes her sound cheery, but I know that's not what it is at all.

Skipping past her comment of never feeling okay, I ask, "Okay, so tell me what all these envelopes and pictures are?"

"There's one for every birthday, the first day of school, her wedding, and more. I tried not to miss an important occasion. I need you to hold onto them and ensure she gets them."

"Wow," I say with saucers for eyes. "This is impressive. How long have you been working on these? Why didn't you tell me? I have so many questions, Olivia."

"You're off track, Hazel," Olivia says, looking worn out but serious.

"Sorry. Okay, so why are you giving these to me? Why not Jett?"

"Because I want you to be *that* person in May's life," she says, pointing at me, then quickly adds, "You've been with me through all of this. You were there at my first doctor's appointment when I found out I was pregnant, and you were there again when I received the news about the cancer. I trust you with my life because you've always been my rock. Your unwavering support means the world to me. I know that no matter what happens, you'll be *that* person for May, loving and protecting her with the same fierce devotion you've always shown me. You're my anchor, Hazel, and I'm forever grateful for your love."

She looks down at her feet and rubs her palms on the silky comforter.

Olivia's word hit me harder than I expected. My throat tightens, and I'm struggling to hold back the tears welling up in my eyes. "I don't know how to do this, Olivia?" My voice cracks. "I love you. I don't want to let go of you, but I know I will have to. I don't know how to live life without you." I take a deep breath feeling Olivia's eyes on me, but I can't meet her gaze.

The door flies open just then, making us both jump. Kadin stands there staring at us. "Should I come back?" she asks, heaving herself onto the bed with us.

"No, Hazel is just being an emotional mess."

"Yeah, she's been like this since she found out this cousin of hers is sick," she says as she kisses us both on the forehead.

"Let's go. We have no plans that include a pity party for poor Hazel," Kadin declares, motioning toward the door. She barely pauses before asking, "Where's my baby?"

"She's with Jett's mom," Olivia says, absently playing with a strand of her hair.

Kadin raises her eyebrow, glancing around. "Where's Jett?"

"In San Diego with Hayes. He has a game tomorrow! Do you ever listen when people talk to you, Kadin? How did you make it almost four years in college without a parent to tell you what was happening?" I ask.

"I didn't need my parents; I had you two." She laughs. "But, seriously, why am I supposed to know they're down there?"

"Because we're all going down for the game tomorrow."

This statement causes Kadin to side-eye me, her lips pursed.

"What?" I say, my hands up in surrender.

Kadin sighs and rubs her temples. "I had plans tomorrow."

Olivia tilts her head and asks, "With who?"

I try to ignore the pang in my chest as I look between them, but I can't help the tightness that creeps up on me. Why do I feel so wounded by hearing Kadin say she has plans? Who does she have plans with? Is she replacing us? Why didn't she tell me? The questions rattle around in my head as I fidget with my phone, scrolling through it to find the proof I had already told her about the game. "I texted you last week to tell you about the game."

Olivia repeats her question, a deep line appearing on her forehead. "Who do you have plans with?"

Kadin shifts uncomfortably, her gaze dropping to the floor. "It doesn't matter," she mutters, barely meeting Olivia's eyes. "Looks like I'll be at Jett's football game." The disappointment in her voice is unmistakable.

We all exchange a glance, feeling the weight of the unspoken tension hanging in the air. The moment lingers, and then, as if reading the room, Olivia breaks the silence. "Will you promise me that once I'm gone, you'll stop denying Hayes proposed to you and marry him already?"

I blink, stunned "No!" I shout, throwing a glance upwards as if seeking an answer from the ceiling. "Well, maybe," I add with a shrug. "I don't know; I've loved him since we were kids, and now that he wants to spend forever with me, I'm not sure I believe him. I'm not sure he knows what he really wants." Looking down to the floor now I say, "I'm just giving him time to change his mind. Because he always does."

"Are you fucking serious?" Kadin screams. "Hayes loves you, you stupid ass. Marry that man before you push him away!"

"Hazel, do not use me as an excuse to sabotage the one thing you've wanted your entire life," Olivia scolds.

"Maybe we can go Vegas, and you can get hitched there," Kadin's eyes are bright with excitement as she bounces on the bed.

"Ummm, hell no. My mother would kill us."

"Your dad would thank us," Kadin says putting her hands out as if she's balancing scales in each hand.

# Chapter 35

## OLIVIA

It's one of those overcast days where the light barely filters though my blinds, making the world feel quieter than usual. I've been in bed for hours, too tired to do anything but lie here. A knock on my door pulls me out of my thoughts.

"Come in," I say, though I know it's my mom and seeing me like this will worry her.

"You're still in bed?" my mom says, but it's not a question if I'm still in bed; it's a question of *why* I'm still in bed.

"I'm just tired, Mom," I try to reassure her, though I can see the worry in her eyes.

"Where's Jett?" she asks, moving more into my room.

"He's helping Hayes at the gym this week. They're running a camp for middle school kids," I explain, though it feels like the energy it takes to speak is just draining me further.

"Where's May?" she asks, looking around my room like I lost my child.

"Dad took her to lunch with Aunt Harper."

"You know your aunt didn't want any kids, but look at her now," she says with a smile. "Every opportunity she gets, she's got your baby wrapped in her arms." Saying this aloud brings my mom visible happiness, and for just a minute the heaviness in the room lifts.

"Yeah, well, babies change people. Look at Hazel when we went to opening day; she volunteered to keep May with her so Jett and I could have a night alone."

"Did she keep her?"

"Yes, but not until May fell asleep, and I knew she'd be down for the night."

"And, look at Jett," my mom adds. Who would've thought that boy that used to chase you on the playground in elementary school and sneak in your window in high school would end up being such an amazing dad?"

"You knew about that?" I ask, full of surprise.

"Baby girl. Have you always taken me for a fool? I knew everything you girls did growing up. I was no angel, you know."

"I love you, Mom. Thank you for letting me grow up knowing it was okay to make mistakes and that no matter what, you'd still love me."

"I love you too, Olivia, more than you'll ever know. You have always been my everything."

Deciding to quickly change the subject before I send my mom to her room in tears, I ask, "Hey, Mom, have you seen my white running shoes? I was going to go out for a walk."

My mom tilts her head and studies me. "Olivia, you donated those last month with our donation pile. Jett bought you red and black custom ones to match his."

"Oh, yeah, I knew I had those," I say, opening my closet door and rummaging through a pile of shoes. "I guess I just forget donating the others. I'll grab the new ones."

My mom watches me, her forehead creased with concern.

"Are you sure you feel okay, babe?" she asks, stepping closer and resting a hand on my arm.

"Yes, Mom, I'm fine," I reply, taking a deep breath and straightening up the pile of shoes. "I'm going to go out, and I'll be back in half an hour."

She hesitates, folding her arms across her chest. "Should I come too?"

"No," I say, gently shaking my head. "I'd like to be alone, if that's okay?"

She nods slowly, her worry evident. "I understand," she murmurs, taking a step back. "Be careful and take your phone."

It's beautiful this time of year in our neighborhood, perched on the precipice of fall, just at the backend of summer. The days are still warm, giving way to cooler nights, but today, with the overcast sky, it feels more reminiscent of fall. The trees are beginning to shed vibrant leaves and the crisp air hints at the season's full arrival. Fall in California is warmer than Texas, a season where you can still enjoy short sleeves and light sweater, the perfect blend of comfort and warmth. The breeze is gentle and the sun, when it's not hidden behind the clouds, casts a golden hue over everything.

Just half a mile north of our house lies an empty grass area with a powerful fountain that gives the feeling of drizzling rain.

Little kids play t-ball there and soccer on the grassy field. I enjoy walking May here in her stroller to watch them. Past the grassy area, a path leads through a mile of towering, mature trees that have stood the test of time in nature.

Two benches hide in the middle of the tree-lined path, offering refuge to those who seek it. Today, the walk here has me a bit winded, so I take the opportunity to find solace in the midst of nature and let my mind rest. I lower myself onto the bench and rest my head on the backrest. Running my hand across the armrest, I'm surprised by how smooth it feels despite enduring countless weather chances. The warmth of the wood seeps into my legs, spreading a comforting sensation throughout my body. Closing my eyes, I focus solely on the sounds around me.

Laughter and playful chatter of children echo in the distance, mingling with the gentle swaying of leaves in the breeze. The birds' melodies fill the air, reminiscent of my moments of solitude in an empty house.

"Olivia!"

"Olivia!"

"*Olivia*!" My dad's deep, panicked voice rings out.

I try to respond, but no words come out as I struggle to answer.

I hear his frantic footsteps coming my way. I'm still frozen, sheltered by the trees.

"Olivia! Are you okay?" His voice trembles with distress as he falls to his knees and shakes me urgently.

Opening my eyes slowly, I meet his gaze, still unable to speak, overtaken by an unfamiliar feeling of grogginess.

As I attempt to close my eyes again, the gentle wind brushes against my face, with each soft gust bringing me an over-whelming sense of peace.

"Olivia, open your eyes," he pleads, clasping my hand tightly in his.

I try to speak but fail, so I squeeze his hand in mine, conveying my emotions.

Leaning closer, he whispers, "Olivia, what's wrong? Tell me, please."

Struggling to form words, I whisper, "I love you, Dad. Take care of Mom and May."

# Chapter 36

## HARPER

People handle heartbreak in their own ways. Hazel screams and cries. Xavier draws into himself, and Joy—well, she's completely withdrawn from reality. As for me, I will deal with my heartbreak in private with Gabe; however, I can't do that until I'm certain everything is handled.

A day has passed since Xavier found Olivia on the bench, and I know I need to check on Joy. Hazel is at home with Gabe and Hayes, who are doing their best to console her. She knows the story of how I lost my cousin when I was just a few years younger than she is. I don't have much else to offer her outside of me telling her I know how she feels, and although it doesn't feel like it now, this ache will grow lighter and lighter with every sunrise. I also know that is the last thing my daughter is open to hearing right now.

Walking up the four steps to Joy and Xavier's front door takes more effort than the thousand other times. The window blinds are closed, not one window allowing an outsider a view into the reality I'm about to walk into.

Opening the front door, I'm flooded with memories of a

baby Olivia crawling to greet us, a young Olivia yelling to her parents, "Hazel is here", and a grouchy teenage Olivia offering nothing more than a wave as she opens the door. All of them are a dagger to my heart, but I'm going to tamp down all my emotions so I can be here for my family.

"Xavier, it's me. Are you here?" I yell from the entryway.

"I'm in my office." His voice is defeated and tired, and my cousin is nothing but a shell of a man right now.

Standing at the door, I just look at him. There are no words for something like this, so we stare at each other, and a silent conversation passes between us.

"Where's Joy?" I ask, breaking the silence.

"Upstairs," he answers with a head jerk in the direction of the stairs.

"How are Nolen and Jensen?" I ask.

He nods slowly. "They're quiet," he says, his voice subdued.

"Gabe is going to pick them up in a few hours and take them somewhere."

"I know, he texted me," he replies, his tone tired and eyes weary.

"Where's May?" I ask, looking around.

"Jett has her at his mom's house."

"Do you need anything before I go see Joy?"

He answers me with a silent shake of his head, and I turn to leave his office.

"Harper," he calls out to me.

Turning back around and walking further into his office, I say, "I know, Xavier."

He stands and pulls me into a hug, his head buried in my shoulder despite him being a good five inches taller than me. His voice trembles as he speaks, "I'm so thankful I was able to hold her hand as she passed, but I don't think I'll ever be okay."

His body shakes slightly, and I wrap my arms tighter around

him, trying to offer any comfort I can. "Xavier," I whisper. "You were there for her when she needed you most."

"But I never took her to dinner," he says, his voice cracking. "Remember? You suggested I take her out, just the two of us. I kept putting it off, thinking there would be time. I thought I had more time." He lets out a shaky breath, pulling back slightly to look at me, his eyes glossy with unshed tears.

"I know," I whisper, my own voice barely steady. "Olivia knew how much you loved her."

"Go see Joy," he says, releasing me.

As I walk through the living room to the stairs leading to their bedroom, I open a few windows, allowing the sun to fill the house. The walls on the way up the stairs are adorned with pictures of Olivia, Nolen and Jensen, telling stories of their adolescent adventures. Pictures of the boys playing football and Olivia in her softball uniform.

I lightly tap Joy's door and push it open, not expecting her to answer or to welcome me in. Quietly, I walk over to where she's lying in bed, her back to me. I remove my shoes before gently pulling the covers back and sliding into bed behind her, drawing her closer. At my touch, I feel her immediate sobs, so instead of speaking, I simply hold her tighter against me, letting her cry until she falls asleep.

## Chapter 37

KADIN

After Hazel's completed her speech, it's my turn. I didn't want to speak today, but I know I have to, because Olivia would have done it for me.

I stand from my aisle seat, my heart pounding. Each step feels heavy as if the weight of my grief is pulling me down. As I make my way to the front, I reach out and grab Hazel's hand as we cross paths. Her dad had to go on stage and lead her back to her seat because she wouldn't leave Olivia's coffin. Hazel walks with her head low, her eyes avoiding contact, tears glistening on her cheeks. Her pain mirrors mine, but I can't let it show.

I walk to the stage with my shoulders back and my head held high. Each step is a silent promise to Olivia. She was my best friend, and she deserves my strength, my courage, my love. The room feels stifling, filled with the muted sounds of quiet sobs and the oppressive weight of sorrow.

As I stand before the podium, I take a deep breath, steadying myself. My legs tremble slightly, but I will them to hold firm. I look out at the sea of faces, all touched by the same grief, and feel a wave of emotion threaten to overwhelm me. But I can't falter. Not now.

I begin to speak, my voice trembling at first, but gaining strength with each word.

"Olivia was…" I correct myself, "No, Olivia *is* the brightest light in all our lives. Her spirit, her laughter, her love, they live on in each of us."

The words flow, each one a testament to our bond. As I speak, I feel her presence, guiding me and giving me the strength to honor her memory the way she deserved.

Tears blur my vision, but I don't stop. My voice grows steadier, infused with the love and admiration I hold for her.

"Olivia taught me what it means to live fully, to love deeply, and to be brave in the face of life's challenges. And today, I stand here, trying to be as brave as she always was."

$$\bullet \quad \bullet \quad \bullet$$

## HAZEL

After the burial, and everyone has made their way to my parent's house for the celebration of life, I just sit at Olivia's grave and watch the groundkeepers finish covering her with dirt and grass.

"Hazel," My dad calls from where our car is parked, walking over to where I'm rooted in place.

I look over at him, not saying anything, trying to hold it together.

He reaches out pulling me into a tight hug, his chin resting on the top of my head. "Let's go; we need to get to the house."

"I'm not coming," I mumble into his chest. "Go ahead without me."

He pulls back slightly to look at me, his forehead creased in concern. "Hazel. It's time."

"Dad, you go," I insist, shaking my head as I stop back. "I'll figure out a way home."

For a minute, he looks like he wants to argue, but he just nods, his hand lingering on my arm for a second longer before he turns to leave.

I watch as he opens the car door for my mom, and she lowers herself into the passenger seat. He closes the door and pauses, his eye meeting mine. I offer him a nod, a silent promise, reassuring him I'll be okay. My mom watches our interaction through the window, her gaze lingering on me as he moves toward the driver's side. A tortured smile curves her lips, its meaning evident – a mixture of apology and understanding. It's a look that says, 'I'm here, but I won't intrude on your grief'. I reply with a slight wave, acknowledging her unspoken promise not to suffocate with my expectations of normalcy. She places her hand against the glass of the passenger window as they drive away.

. . .

I'm gently shaken awake, surprised. I open my eyes and see Hayes kneeling next to me.

"What are you doing here?" I ask, trying to straighten my hair.

"Why are you still here, Hazel? The funeral has been over for hours, and it's almost dark. I don't think the answer to all this is sleeping alone in a graveyard."

"I must've fallen asleep, that's it."

"Hazel, I'll sit with you all night if you don't want to leave, but you can't stay here alone. If you're ready to go home, I'll come back with you tomorrow, the next day, and the next, but you have to know that Olivia isn't here, and she wouldn't want you here either."

"I can't say goodbye to her, and I don't know how to live without Olivia."

"We all have to live without someone, Hazel. Olivia is your first someone." He stands as he says this and extends his hand to me.

I take it, and he gently lifts me up, brushing off my black dress as I stand in front of him.

He takes me in his arms and holds me there, not allowing me to push him away. I turn my head and rest my cheek against his chest, finally allowing myself a deep breath. His scent mingles with the fragrance of the flowers and freshly cut grass, offering me just a moment of comfort amidst my pain.

"I need to get you home, Hazel."

# Chapter 38

<br>

## HARPER

I've always said my daughter is a tiny version of me, until one day, she wasn't; she was just herself. I watched my daughter grieve the death of her best friend and cousin just like I did all those years ago. The most significant difference is that Hazel didn't let Olivia's death define her as I did for many years. I became a shell of a human, but Hazel is determined to keep moving forward. Just like I thought she would.

Hazel and Hayes were married on the second anniversary of Olivia's death because she and Olivia made a promise that Hazel wouldn't dwell on her death but celebrate her life. May walked down the aisle wearing a puffy white dress with layers and layers of tulle, similar to the one her mom wore when she married Jett. She shamelessly threw handfuls of flowers into the audience with no regard for wedding etiquette, and I wouldn't have it any other way.

As for me, I'm eagerly waiting to start the third chapter of my life. The first chapter began when I met and fell in love with Gabe; the second unfolded as I became a mother. But knowing I'll be a grandmother any day now fills me with a *joy greater than anything I've ever felt.*

*Reflecting on my journey, I'm so happy my life turned out the way it did. I'm profoundly grateful that Gabe fought for us every day and forgave me when I treated him unforgivably. And I feel incredibly fortunate that we accidentally got pregnant with Hazel. Without her, not only would my life be less vibrant, but I'd also feel an emptiness I can't even fathom.*

*Do I wish things were different for Xavier and Joy? Of course I do. My poor cousin lost his brother at twenty years old and now his daughter. I can't even imagine the heartbreak he's hiding, trying to be strong for Joy, the twins, and little May. But that's Xavier—the second-best man you'll ever meet.*

"Mom, Mom, Mom."

"I'll be right down, Hazel; I'm just writing in my journal."

"Mom, my water broke. We *have* to go *now!*"

• • •

## JOY

*It seems appropriate that I have the final say, especially considering Harper had the first word. However, that sentiment feels incomplete without delving into the story of Harper and Gabe. Without their story, would I have mine? I often ponder the distrust and dislike Harper and I once shared for one another, and now I can't imagine functioning without her. The transformation of our relationship from animosity to a deep bond is something I reflect on often, realizing how essential it has become to my life.*

*She was there for me when Olivia passed. She didn't push to move forward; she laid with me every day while I broke,* and then she cheered me on while I put myself together.

A part of my soul died with Olivia that day, but circumstances kept me alive. Two years later, some days, I still wish I could trade places with her, but her ending wasn't intended for my ending, and I know I'll never understand how the universe works.

We buried Olivia next to my grandma. She was convinced my grandma would be waiting for her in heaven, so it's only fitting if they'll spend eternity together there as well.

If I said I handled Olivia's death with dignity, I'd be lying. It took me months to get out of bed, and I nearly pushed my husband away when he showed me some tough love for the sake of our twins. I was so trapped by my sorrow that I forgot about the two amazing young men who still very much needed their mother in the wake of losing their older sister. And Xavier— how does a man who lost his brother at a young age and now his daughter cope? He is strong, showing nothing but resilience and grace in heartbreak.

The one amazing thing I have left is my granddaughter. She has Olivia's blue eyes and a round, beautiful face. Unknowingly, in typical fashion, Olivia gave all of us the greatest gift ever—a shared grandbaby.

Olivia left behind so many memories of the wonderful human she was, but she also kept a journal for the last two years of her life. Pages filled with her thoughts and fears, a notebook littered with love letters meant for her father and me, and her wishes for her daughter, but most importantly, her wishes for Jett.

• • •

*Jett,*

*I've entrusted letters for May to Hazel. They're for important occasions that I won't be there for. She'll find one for every birthday, first day of school, first heartbreak, her wedding day, and birth of her first child. Please work with Hazel to see that she receives them.*

*I've also left several framed pictures of us. Keep them in her room only. Most importantly, please don't hold onto the past. Don't let guilt keep you stuck. Start a new chapter. Our daughter will need a mom, and you'll need a wife (trust me, you need a wife. LOL).*

*Jett, I may be gone, but you're still here. Don't stop living. Show our daughter all the things I wanted to.*

*Love Always,*
*Olivia*

*PS – I fell in love with you the first day I saw you in kindergarten. Xx forever*

• • •

*Is all lost? I guess that depends on how you look at things. Xavier gave me one of the best friends I could ever ask for in Harper, and because of Harper, I have Hazel, who will never let Olivia's memory fade. Olivia, well, she made me a mother and a grandma.*

*Is this the Happily Ever After I dreamed of growing up? No, it's not, but who really gets their dream ending? I met Xavier by chance circumstances. A man that I never deserved. I survived a horrific car accident that left me paralyzed for a year. He refused to leave my side. A year in, he proved to me that no circumstance this universe throws at us would be too much for us to overcome. I can hold onto my sorrow forever or choose to let it go.*

*Accept that there can still be a happy ending despite death and heartbreak. I have two amazing young men who I continue to watch grow into amazing men like their father. I have an amazing granddaughter, who I get to watch grow up with my best friend Roxanne, and Harper, who has always been part of my family. And, my husband, who casually flirted with me in my apartment building so many years ago, bought a car not from his cousin but from me so that he could take me to dinner. So, all in all, I think I'm one fortunate person.*

"Joy!"

"I'll be right down, Xavier; I'm writing in my journal."

"It's Hazel, her water broke. Everyone is on their way to the hospital. We have to go now.

# *Epilogue*

May

"**S**urprise!" echoes through the house as soon as I open the front door, the sound almost knocking me back from the unexpected volume.

I freeze, eyes wide, taking in the sight before me. Our living room is decorated with pink and gold balloons floating in every corner. Streamers crisscross the ceiling, and a huge 'Sweet Sixteen' banner stretches across the wall.

Today is my sixteenth birthday, and I can't help but hope for the ultimate gift - a shiny new car sitting in the garage with a big red bow.

Our house is filled with everyone who is special to me. Dad and my bonus mom, Kadin, treated my cousin Olivia and me to a birthday dinner, keeping me blissfully unaware of what was happening back home. It was all part of Aunt Hazel's plan, giving her the time she needed to put together this surprise birthday for me.

With my dad and Kadin leading the way, we head to the garage, my excitement barely contained.

Kadin was one of my biological mom's best friends. She adopted me shortly after she and my dad got married. My biological mom (Olivia, not to be confused with my cousin, who is named in memory of her) passed away from a cancerous brain tumor shortly after my first birthday. While I don't remember her, I cherish the pictures of the two of us and the videos she left behind. She spent the last few months of her life bedridden, and during that time, she poured her heart into writing letters to me. I have opened one on every birthday. Each one a treasure trove of her love and advice. Even when a recent breakup broke my heart, there was a letter waiting to comfort me. She (and my Aunt Hazel, who holds all the letters) didn't miss any life events, and I can only imagine there are several more letters yet to come.

My Aunt Hazel, Uncle Hayes, Kadin, and Dad talk about her often, recalling stories and memories in our casual conversations. Their stories paint such a vivid picture of who she was that I feel like I know her intimately, making me miss her even though I never knew her.

We all make our way out to the garage, and I'm greeted with a surprise I've only dreamed of – a brand-new car!

"Check the backseat," my dad says, opening the driver's side door for me.

In the backseat, is my mom's softball bat from when she played in high school. Attached is a sealed envelope with a sticker that reads '*Sweet Sixteen*'. The envelope is written in my mom's familiar handwriting: '*To my beautiful daughter. Love always: Your Mom.*'

I tuck the letter into the back pocket of my high-waisted faded jeans to read later in the quiet privacy of my bedroom. These are the few moments when I have my mom all to myself. It's where she and I make our own memories, though it's through her words and my voice only; they are sacred to me, and I treasure the tradition that brings us together, bridging the distance between the heavens and my bedroom.

Also available

from Kara Jefferies...

# a girl named Harper

KARA JEFFERIES

# Chapter 1

## GABE

Stepping out of the elevator and into the dimly lit parking garage, I squint as my eyes adjust to the sunlight, trying to sneak in from outside. The sound of my brown boots echoes against the concrete as I make my way toward my car. As I approach, something catches my eye—a vehicle parked crookedly across two spaces, engine still running. My heart skips a beat when I recognize it. It's hers. The girl I've been fantasizing about since I saw her moving in last week by herself, one box at a time. I thought about offering to help, but something held me back. Maybe it's because I don't like to linger when 'visiting Joy'.

We have an understanding, Joy and me—friends with benefits, nothing more, nothing less. We don't do dates or romantic dinners. We hang out, we fuck, and that's where we draw the line. We agreed right at the beginning that if one of us ever started catching feelings, we'd end it – no drama, no complications.

I hurry over to her car, concern gripping me. She's slumped against the seat, eyes half-closed. I knock on the window, but she barely stirs. Panic surges through me as I open the door.

"Hey, are you okay?" I ask, my voice urgent but gentle.

She mumbles something, her words slurred and barely audible. "Yeah…just tired," she manages, her eyes fluttering as she attempts to focus on me.

My concern ratches up a hundred notches as I notice the pill bottle on the passenger seat. I grab for it and read the label. Sleeping pills. "Did you…take these?" I ask, my voice overflowing with worry.

"No, no…just resting," she mumbles, her head lolling to the side.

My heart pounds as I realize how out of it she really is. "You need medical attention," I say, but she shakes her head.

"I'm fine…just need to sleep," she insists, though her words are barely coherent.

Standing next to her car with the door open. I watch her struggle to stay coherent. It's really none of my business, this girl isn't my concern, I remind myself. But, a sense of responsibility washes over me. I can't, in good conscience, leave her alone in this parking garage—no matter how much she insists on being left alone.

Without another word, I reach into her car, unbuckle her seatbelt, and gently scoop her into my arms. She protests weakly, her head resting against my chest, "I'm fine, really…"

I reply, my voice steady as I carry her toward the elevator, "You're in no shape to be out here."

She mumbles something about putting her down so she can walk on her own, all while nuzzling herself into the warmth of my chest. I find myself appreciating the gesture, even if I don't want to admit it.

I reach her apartment and, the awkwardness of balancing her while trying to unlock the door forces me to adjust my approach. I gently set her down, supporting her against the wall. She murmurs something unintelligible, her head lolling slightly as she fights to keep her eyes open.

I turn to her purse, which hangs off her shoulder, its contents a mystery to me. The necessity of the situation doesn't ease the discomfort I feel as I sift through her belongings. My fingers brush against the soft fabric of her wallet, a pack of gum, and then finally, the cold metal of her keys. I pull them out with a slight clink of metal, feeling the invasion of privacy weigh heavy on my conscience.

With the keys now in hand, I scoop Harper back into my arms, cradling her gently. As I insert the key into the lock, I can't help but feel protective yet intrusive.

I carry her inside, before laying her gently on the couch. She mumbles something again, half protest, half thanks, as she curls up, already drifting back to sleep.

I grab a blanket from the nearby chair and cover her, watching her for a moment, making sure she's breathing steadily, before sitting nearby to work out what I'm meant to do now. The responsibility feels heavy. I don't even know this girl, and yet here I am, sitting in her apartment, taking care of her.

**Order your copy here:**
www.amazon.com/Girl-Named-Harper/dp/B0D35SVV2C

# About Kara Jefferies

I write about real characters facing real-life problems. My stories feature women who stumble, swear, and love with everything they've got. My goal is to make you feel—whether that means squirming, laughing, getting mad, or smiling through it all. My version of "happily ever after" may look a little different than yours, and for that, I make no apologies. Life isn't perfect, but there's beauty in the imperfections, and that's what I strive to capture on every page.

Email: Itskaraj39@gmail.com

Kara loves to hear from readers. You can find her contact information, website and author biography at: www.karajefferies.com

# Also by Kara Jefferies

*A Girl Named Harper*

*A Girl Named Joy*

*The Joy of it All*

www.ingramcontent.com/pod-product-compliance
Lightning Source LLC
Chambersburg PA
CBHW020758310726
48969CB00002B/593